Grace Harlowe's Third Year at Overton College

Jessie Graham Flower

Esprios.com

Grace Harlowe's Third Year at Overton College

The College Girls Series

Jessie Graham Flower, A.M.

Grace Harlowe's Third Year at Overton College

By JESSIE GRAHAM FLOWER, A. M.

Author of The Grace Harlowe High School Girls Series, Grace Harlowe's First Year at Overton College, Grace Harlowe's Second Year at Overton College, Grace Harlowe's Fourth Year at Overton College.

PHILADELPHIA
HENRY ALTEMUS COMPANY

1914

The Eight Originals Were Spending a Last Evening Together.

CONTENTS

CHAPTER I. The Last Evening at Home
CHAPTER II. The Arrival of Kathleen
CHAPTER III. First Impressions
CHAPTER IV. Getting Acquainted with the Newspaper Girl
CHAPTER V. Two Is a Company
CHAPTER VI. An Unsuspected Listener
CHAPTER VII. An Unpleasant Summons
CHAPTER VIII. Elfreda Prophecies Trouble
CHAPTER IX. Opening the Bazaar
CHAPTER X. The Alice in Wonderland Circus
CHAPTER XI. Grace Meets With a Rebuff
CHAPTER XII. Thanksgiving at Overton
CHAPTER XIII. Arline Makes the Best of a Bad Matter
CHAPTER XIV. Planning the Christmas Dinner
CHAPTER XV. A Tissue Paper Tea
CHAPTER XVI. A Doubtful Victory
CHAPTER XVII. Hippy Looks Mysterious
CHAPTER XVIII. Old Jean's Story
CHAPTER XIX. Telling Ruth the News
CHAPTER XX. Elfreda Realizes Her Ambition
CHAPTER XXI. Alberta Keeps Her Promise
CHAPTER XXII. Grace's Plan
CHAPTER XXIII. What Emma Dean Forgot
CHAPTER XXIV. Conclusion

LIST OF ILLUSTRATIONS

The Eight Originals Were Spending a Last Evening Together.

The Emerson Twins Looked Realistically Japanese.

"Here is the Letter You Wrote the Dean."

"She was Standing Close to the Door."

CHAPTER I

THE LAST EVENING AT HOME

"Now, then, everyone join in the chorus," commanded Hippy Wingate. There was an answering tinkle from Reddy's mandolin, the deeper notes of a guitar sounded, then eight care-free young voices were raised in the plaintive chorus of "My Old Kentucky Home."

It was a warm night in September. Miriam Nesbit and seven of the Eight Originals were spending a last evening together on the Harlowes' hospitable veranda. They were on the eve of separation. The following day would witness Nora's and Jessica's departure for the conservatory. Grace and Miriam would return to Overton at the beginning of the next week, and the latter part of the same week would find the four young men entered upon their senior year in college.

"Very fine, indeed," commented Hippy, "but in order to sing properly one ought to drink a great deal of lemonade. It is very conducive to a grand opera voice," he added, confiscating several cakes from the plate Grace passed to him and holding out his empty lemonade glass.

"But you haven't a grand opera voice," protested David. "That is only a flimsy excuse."

"We won't discuss the matter in detail," returned Hippy with dignity. "I am prepared to prove the truth of what I say. I will now render a selection from 'Il Trovatore.' I will sing the imprisoned lover's song—"

"Not if I have anything to say about it," growled Reddy.

"Suit yourself, suit yourself," declared Hippy, shrugging his shoulders. "You boys will be sorry if you don't let me sing, though."

"Is that a threat?" inquired Tom Gray with pretended belligerence.

"A threat?" repeated Hippy. "No, it is a fact. I am contemplating a terrible revenge. That is, I haven't really begun to contemplate it yet. I am just getting ready. But when I do start—well, you'll see."

"I think it would be delightful to hear you sing, 'Ah, I Have Sighed to Rest Me,' Hippy," broke in Nora sweetly, a mischievous twinkle in her eyes.

"Can I believe my ears? The stony, unsympathetic Nora O'Malley agrees with me at last. She likes my voice; she wishes to hear me sing, 'Ah, I Have Sighed to Rest Me.' 'Tis true, I *have* sighed to rest me a great many times, particularly in the morning when the alarm clock put an end to my dreams. It is a beautiful selection."

"Then, why not sing it?" asked Nora demurely.

"Because I don't know it," replied Hippy promptly.

"Just as I suspected," commented Nora in disgust. "That is precisely why I asked you to sing."

"What made you suspect me?" inquired Hippy, apparently impressed.

"I suspected you on general principles," was the retort.

"If you had had any general principles you wouldn't have suspected me," parried Hippy.

"I won't even think about you the next time," was the withering reply. Nora rose and made her way to the other end of the veranda, perching on the porch railing beside Tom Gray.

"Come back, Nora," wailed Hippy. "You may suspect me."

"Isn't he too ridiculous for anything?" whispered Nora, smothering a giggle and trying to look severe. Her attempt failed ignominiously when Hippy, with an exaggeratedly contrite expression on his fat face, sidled up to her, salaamed profoundly, lost his balance and sprawled on all fours at her feet. A shout of merriment arose from his friends. Hippy, unabashed, scrambled to his feet and began bowing again before Nora, this time taking care not to bend too far forward.

"You are forgiven, Hippy," declared Miriam. "Nora, don't allow your old friend and playmate to dislocate his spine in his efforts to show his sorrow."

"You may stop bowing," said Nora grudgingly. "I suppose I'll have to forgive you."

Hippy promptly straightened up and perched himself on the railing beside Nora.

"I didn't say you might sit here," teased Nora.

"I know it," replied Hippy coolly. "Still, you would be deeply, bitterly disappointed if I didn't."

"Perhaps I should," admitted Nora. "I suppose you might as well stay," she added with affected carelessness.

"Thank you," retorted Hippy. "But I had made up my mind not to move."

"Had you?" said Nora indifferently, turning her back on Hippy and addressing Tom Gray. Whereupon Hippy raised his voice in a loud monologue that entirely drowned Tom's and Nora's voices.

"For goodness' sake, say something that will please him, Nora," begged Tom. "This is awful."

Hippy babbled on, apparently oblivious of everyone.

"I have something very important to tell you, Hippy," interposed Nora slyly.

Hippy stopped talking. "What is it?" he asked suspiciously.

"Come over to the other end of the veranda and find out," said Nora enigmatically.

Hippy accepted the invitation promptly, and followed Nora to the end of the veranda, unmindful of Tom Gray's jeers about idle curiosity.

Those who read "Grace Harlowe's Plebe Year at High School," "Grace Harlowe's Sophomore Year at High School," "Grace Harlowe's Junior Year at High School" and "Grace Harlowe's Senior Year at High School" will have no trouble in recognizing every member of the merry party of young folks who had taken possession of the Harlowes' veranda. The doings of Tom, Hippy, David, Reddy, Nora, Jessica, Anne and Grace have been fully narrated in the "High School Girls Series." There, too, appeared Miriam Nesbit, Eva Allen, Eleanor Savelli and Marian Barber, together with the four chums, as members of the famous sorority, the Phi Sigma Tau.

With the close of their high school days the little clan had been separated, although David, Reddy and Hippy were on the eve of beginning their senior year in the same college. Nora and Jessica were attending the same conservatory, while Grace, Anne and Miriam Nesbit were students at Overton College.

During their freshman year at Overton, set forth in "Grace Harlowe's First Year at Overton College," the three girls had not met with altogether plain sailing. There had been numerous hitches, the most serious one having been caused by their championship of J. Elfreda Briggs, a freshman, who had unfortunately incurred the dislike of several mischievous sophomores. Through the prompt, sensible action of Grace, assisted by her friends, Elfreda was restored to favor by her class and became one of Grace's staunchest friends.

"Grace Harlowe's Second Year at Overton College" found the three friends sophomores, and wholly devoted to Overton and its traditions. Their sophomore days brought them a variety of experiences, pleasant and unpleasant, and, as in their freshman year, Grace and Miriam distinguished themselves on the basketball field. It was during this year that the Semper Fidelis Club was organized for the purpose of helping needy students through college, and that Eleanor Savelli, the daughter of a world-renowned virtuoso, and one of the Phi Sigma Tau, visited Grace and helped to plan a concert which netted the club two hundred dollars and a substantial yearly subscription from an interested outsider. The difficulties that arose over a lost theme and the final outcome of the affair proved Grace Harlowe to be the same honorable, straightforward young woman who had endeared herself to the reader during her high school days.

"Why doesn't some one sing?" asked Grace plaintively. A brief silence had fallen upon the little group at one end of the veranda, broken only by Nora's and Hippy's argumentative voices.

"Because both the someones are too busy to sing," laughed Jessica, casting a significant glance toward the end of the veranda.

"Hippy, Nora," called David, "come over here and sing."

"'Sing, sing, what shall I sing?'" chanted Hippy. "Shall it be a sweetly sentimental ditty, or shall I sing of brooks and meadows, fields and flowers?"

"Sing that funny one you sang for the fellows the night of the Pi Ipsilon dinner," urged David.

"Very well," beamed Hippy. "Remember, to the singer belongs the food. I always negotiate for refreshments before lifting up my voice in song."

"I will see that you are taken care of, Hippy," smiled Mrs. Harlowe, who had come out on the veranda in time to hear Hippy's declaration.

"Hello, Mother dear," called Grace, "I didn't know you were there."

The young people were on their feet in an instant. Grace led her mother to a chair. "Stay with us awhile, Mother," she said. "Hippy is going to sing, and Nora, too."

"Then I shall surely stay," replied Mrs. Harlowe. "And after the songs you must come into the house and be my guests. The table is set for seven."

"How nice in you, Mother!" exclaimed Grace, kissing her mother's cheek. "You are always doing the things that make people happy.

Nora and Hippy, please sing your very best for Mother. You first, Hippy, because I want Nora to sing Tosti's 'Serenata,' and a comic song afterward will completely spoil the effect."

Hippy sang two songs in his own inimitable fashion. Then Nora's sweet, high soprano voice began the "Serenata" to the subdued tinkling accompaniment of Reddy's mandolin. Two years in the conservatory had done much for Nora's voice, though its plaintive sweetness had been her natural heritage. As they listened to the clear, rounded tones, with just a suspicion of sadness in them, the little company realized to a person that Nora's hopes of becoming known in the concert or grand opera world were quite likely to be fulfilled.

"How I wish Anne were here to-night," lamented Grace, after having vigorously applauded Nora's song. "She loves to hear you sing, Nora."

"I know it," sighed Nora. "Dear little Anne! I'm so sorry we can't see her before we go back to the conservatory. While we have been sitting here singing and enjoying ourselves, Anne has been appearing in her farewell performance. I am glad we had a chance to visit her this summer, even though we had to cross the state to do it."

"She will be here to-morrow night, but we shall be at the end of our journey by that time," lamented Jessica. "I wish we might stay and see her, but we can't."

"Never mind, you will meet her at Christmas time, when the Eight Originals gather home," comforted Miriam.

"But we'd like to see her now," interposed David mournfully. "What is Oakdale without Anne?"

At that moment Mrs. Harlowe, who, after Nora's song, had excused herself and gone into the house, appeared in the door.

"Come, children," she smiled, "the feast is spread."

"May I escort you to the table?" asked David gravely, offering her his arm. Heading the little procession, they led the way to the dining room, followed by Reddy and Jessica, Hippy and Nora, Grace, Tom and Miriam.

There for the next hour goodfellowship reigned supreme, and when at last the various members of the little clan departed for home, each one carried in his or her heart the conviction that Life could never offer anything more desirable than these happy evenings which they had spent together.

"I can't tell you how much I missed Anne to-night," said Grace to her mother as, arm in arm, they stood on the veranda watching their guests until they had turned the corner of the next street.

"We all missed her," replied her mother, "but I believe David felt her absence even more keenly than we did. He is very fond of Anne. I wonder if she realizes that he really loves her, and that he will some day tell her so? She is such a quiet, self-contained little girl. Her emotions are all kept for her work."

"I believe she does," said Grace. "She has never spoken of it to me. David has been her faithful knight ever since her freshman year at high school, so she ought to have a faint inkling of what the rest of us know. I am sorry for David. Anne's art is a powerful rival, and she is growing fonder of it with every season. If, after she finishes college, she were to marry David, she would be obliged to give it up. Since the Southards came into her life she has grown to love her profession so dearly that I don't imagine she would sacrifice it even for David's sake."

"It sounds rather strange to hear my little girl talking so wisely of other people's love affairs," smiled Mrs. Harlowe almost wistfully.

"I know what you are thinking, Motherkin," responded Grace, slipping both arms about her mother and drawing her gently into the big porch swing. "You needn't be afraid, though. I don't feel in the least sentimental over any one, not even Tom Gray, and I like him better than any other young man I know. I am far more concerned over what to do once I have finished college. I simply must work, but I haven't yet found my vocation. Neither has Miriam. Jessica thinks she has found hers, but she found Reddy first, and he does not intend that she shall lose sight of him. Hippy and Nora are a great deal fonder of each other than appears on the surface, too. Their disagreements are never private. Nora said the other day that she and Hippy had had only one quarrel, and—this is the funniest bit of news you ever heard, Mother—it was because Hippy became jealous of a violinist Nora knows at the conservatory. Imagine Hippy as being jealous!"

Grace talked on to her mother of her friends and of herself while Mrs. Harlowe listened, thinking happily that she was doubly blessed in not only her daughter, but in having that daughter's confidence as well.

CHAPTER II

THE ARRIVAL OF KATHLEEN

"There is a whole lot in getting accustomed to things," remarked J. Elfreda Briggs sagely, as she stood with a hammer and nail in one hand, a Japanese print in the other, her round eyes scanning the wall for an appropriate place to hang her treasure.

"It's a beauty, isn't it?" declared Miriam, passing over her roommate's remark and looking admiringly at the print, which her roommate had just taken from her trunk.

"What, this?" asked Elfreda. "You'd better believe it is. Goodness knows I paid enough for it. But I wasn't talking about this print. I was talking about our present junior estate. What I wonder is, whether being a junior will go to my head and make me vainglorious or whether I shall wear the honor as a graceful crown," ended the stout girl with an affected smile, which changed immediately to a derisive grin.

"I should say, neither," responded Miriam slyly. "I don't believe anything would ever go to your head. You're too matter-of-fact, and as for your graceful crown, it would be over one ear within half an hour."

Both girls laughed, then Elfreda, having found a spot on the wall that met with her approval, set the nail and began hammering. "There!" she exclaimed with satisfaction. "That is exactly where I want it. Now I can begin to think about something else."

"I wonder why Grace and Anne haven't paid us a call this morning?" mused Miriam, who sat listlessly before her trunk, apparently undecided whether to begin the tedious labor of unpacking or to put it off until some more convenient day.

"I'll go and find them," volunteered Elfreda, dropping her hammer and turning toward the door. "They must be at home." Five minutes later she raced back with the news that their door was locked and the "out indefinitely" sign was displayed.

"That is very strange," pondered Miriam, aloud. "I wonder where they have gone?"

"Why on earth didn't they tell us they were going? That's what I'd like to know," declared Elfreda.

"Perhaps Mrs. Elwood knows something about it," suggested Miriam.

The mere mention of Mrs. Elwood's name caused Elfreda to dart through the hall and downstairs to the living-room in search of the good-natured matron. Failing to find her, she walked through the kitchen to the shady back porch, where Mrs. Elwood sat rocking and reading the newspaper which the newsboy had just brought.

"Oh, Mrs. Elwood," she cried, "have you seen Grace and Anne? We can't find them."

"Didn't Miss Dean tell you?" asked Mrs. Elwood in a surprised tone.

"Miss Dean," repeated Elfreda disgustedly. "No wonder we didn't know what had become of them. With all Emma's estimable qualities, she is the one person I know whom I would not trust to deliver a message. I beg your pardon, Mrs. Elwood, I didn't mean that you were in any sense to blame. We ought to have warned you, only Emma is such a splendid girl that one hates to mention a silly little thing like that. Just forget that I said it, will you?"

Mrs. Elwood smiled. "I quite understand, Miss Briggs," she said gravely. "The message Miss Harlowe left with me was this: 'If the girls ask where we have gone, tell them that we received a telegram and had to go to the station. All explanations when we come back.'"

"That settles it," groaned Elfreda. "We know only enough to whet our curiosity. And we can't find out more unless we follow them to the station. We can't do that, either. It would not look well. Besides, we are not invited." Elfreda had been rapidly reflecting aloud, much to Mrs. Elwood's amusement. "I'll have to go back and tell Miriam," she finished.

"But why did they lock their door?" asked Miriam, when Elfreda had repeated her information.

"I don't know," returned Elfreda thoughtfully. "Yes, I do know!" she exclaimed with sudden inspiration. "I think Grace was afraid she might have a repetition of last year's performance."

"'Last year's performance,'" repeated Miriam in a puzzled tone.

"Yes, don't you remember the Anarchist?" retorted Elfreda, with a reminiscent grin.

"Of course!" exclaimed Miriam, laughing a little at the recollection. "Wasn't she formidable, though, when she slammed the door in our faces?"

Elfreda nodded. "She is all right now. At least she was when she visited me. I never saw a girl blossom and expand as she did. Pa liked her. He thought she was smart. She is, too. She has lived so entirely with that scientific father of hers that she has absorbed all sorts of odds and ends of knowledge from him. That is why college and girls and the whole thing terrified her."

"Terrified her," said Miriam incredulously. "I thought matters quite the reverse."

"That was precisely what I thought until she told me that, no matter how vengeful she looked, she was always afraid of the girls. She never seemed to be able to say the right thing at the right moment. That was why she used to scowl so fiercely when any one spoke or looked at her."

"I don't think it was altogether fear of the girls that caused her to lock us out that day," observed Miriam, a gleam of laughter appearing in her black eyes.

"I don't suppose it was," retorted Elfreda good-humoredly. "She says she knows her disposition to be anything but angelic. But she is trying, Miriam. You wait and see for yourself how the new Laura Atkins behaves."

"But to go back to the subject of the door, what makes you think Grace locked it on account of last year?" persisted Miriam.

"Oh, I don't know," answered Elfreda vaguely. "I just thought so, that's all."

"We'll ask her when she comes, just for fun," declared Miriam. "Why not go downstairs and sit on the back veranda with Mrs. Elwood? We can hear the girls as soon as they come into the yard."

"All right," agreed Elfreda. "Do you care if I take my magazine along? I am not quite through with an article I began this morning."

"I object seriously," smiled Miriam. "I shall expect you to entertain me. You can finish reading your article later."

Elfreda glanced up quickly from the magazine she held in her hand. Then, catching sight of her friend's smiling face, she tucked her magazine under one arm, linked her free arm through Miriam's and marched her toward the stairs. They had reached the foot of the stairs and were half way down the hall when the sound of voices caused both girls to stand still, listening intently.

"That sounds like Grace's voice!" exclaimed Elfreda. With one accord they turned about, hurrying to the veranda at the front of the house in time to see Grace and Anne approaching. Both girls were laden with luggage, while between them walked an alert little figure, tugging a bag of golf sticks, a fat, black leather hand bag and a camera.

"What manner of woman have we here?" muttered Elfreda, regarding the newcomer with quizzical eyes.

But before Miriam found time to reply the newcomer set her luggage in the middle of the walk, and running up to Miriam and Elfreda, said with a frank laugh: "This is Miriam and this is Elfreda. You see I know both of you from Mabel's description."

"Who—what—" began Elfreda.

"Girls," said Grace, who had by this time come up with the animated stranger, "this is Miss West, a friend of Mabel Ashe's. My telegram was from Mabel asking me to meet Miss West, and as Anne and I were on the porch when it came, and the train we were to meet was due, we didn't stop for explanations or hats, but raced down the street as fast as we could go."

While Grace was talking, Kathleen West was shaking hands vigorously with Miriam and Elfreda. "I'm so glad to know you," she said, "and I think I'm going to like you. I'm not so sure about liking college, even though I've worked so hard to get here. I hope to goodness I don't flunk in the exams."

"I am sure that any friend of Mabel's is bound to be ours also," said Miriam courteously. She had not made up her mind regarding the newcomer.

"Thank you. From what she said I should imagine that you and she were on very good terms," returned the stranger lightly. "Of course you know who I am and all about me."

Grace smiled. "Not yet, but we are willing to hear anything you wish to tell us."

"Oh, that's so!" exclaimed the stranger. "Mabel wrote about me, but her letter hasn't reached you yet, and, of course, telegrams can't be very lengthy unless you wish to spend a fortune or the office has a franchise. There I go again about the office. I might as well tell the truth and have done with it: I'm a newspaper woman."

CHAPTER III

FIRST IMPRESSIONS

Miriam smiled involuntarily, Grace looked surprised, Elfreda indifferent, and Anne amused. The word "woman" seemed absurdly out of place from the lips of this girl who looked as though she had just been promoted to long dresses.

"Oh, yes, I know I look not more than eighteen," quickly remarked Kathleen West, noticing Miriam's smile. "But I'm not. I'm twenty-two years old, and I've been on a newspaper for four years. Why, that's the way I earned my money to come here. I'll tell you about it some other time. It's too long a story for now. Besides, I'm hungry. At what time are we to be fed and are the meals good? I have no illusions regarding boarding houses."

"The meals are excellent," replied Anne. "You must have dinner with us. Then we will see about securing a room for you. I think you will be able to get in here. This used to be considered a freshman house, but all those who were freshmen with us have stayed on, and if last year's freshmen stay, too, then Wayne Hall will be full and—"

"I won't get in," finished the young woman calmly.

"Come into the house now and meet Mrs. Elwood," invited Grace. "Then you can learn your fate."

"Yes, I can just make room for you," Mrs. Elwood was saying a few minutes later. "Miss Evans is not coming back, and Miss Acker is going to Livingstone Hall. Her two particular friends are there. Miss Dean wishes to room alone this year, so that disposes of the vacancy left by Miss Acker. But the half of the room Miss Evans had is not occupied. It is on the second floor at the east end of the hall."

"Then I'll take it," returned Kathleen promptly, "and move in at once. I may not stay here long, but at least I'll be happy while I stay. But if I should survive all these exams, there will be cause for rejoicing and I'll give a frolic that you will all remember, or my name's not Kathleen West. Is there any one who would love to help me upstairs with my things?"

"Well, what do you think of her?" asked Elfreda abruptly. Having helped Kathleen to her room with her luggage they had left her to herself and were now in their own room. Miriam stood looking out the window, her hands behind her back. At Elfreda's question she turned, looked thoughtfully at her roommate, then said slowly: "I don't know. I haven't decided. She's friendly and enthusiastic and hard and indifferent all in the same moment. I think her work has made her so. I believe she has hidden her inner self away so deep that she has forgotten what the real Kathleen is like."

"I believe so, too, Miriam," agreed Elfreda. "I could see that you weren't favorably impressed with her. I could see—"

"You see entirely too much," laughed Miriam. "I haven't even formed an opinion of Miss West yet. I wonder how long she has known Mabel Ashe? Not very long, I'll wager."

An hour later Grace appeared in the door, waving a letter. "Here's Mabel's letter!" she cried. "Come into my room, and we will read it."

"The letter was not far behind the telegram," remarked Anne, as she closed the door of their room and seated herself on the couch beside Miriam.

"Do hurry, Grace, and read us what Mabel has to offer on the subject of Kathleen Mavourneen—West, I mean," corrected Elfreda with a giggle.

Grace unfolded the letter and began to read:

"MY DEAR GRACE:—

"Please forgive me for neglecting you so shamefully, but I am now wrestling with a real job on a real newspaper and am so occupied with trying to keep it that I haven't had time to think of anything else. Father is deeply disgusted with my journalistic efforts. He wished me to go to Europe this summer, but the light of ambition burns too vividly to be quenched even by my beloved Europe. When next I go abroad it will be with my own hard-earned wages.

"I haven't done anything startling yet; I have been chronicling faithfully the doings of society. As most of the elect are out of town, my news gathering has not been in the nature of a harvest. However, I am still striving, still hoping for the day when I shall leave society far behind and sally forth on the trail of a big story.

"But, I am diverging from one of the chief purposes of this letter. It is to introduce to you Kathleen West, an ambitious and particularly clever young woman, who is a 'star' reporter on this paper. It seems that she and I have changed ambitions. I sigh for journalistic fame, and she sighs for college. She has done more than sigh. She has been saving her money for ever so long, determined to take unto herself a college education. I admire her spirit and have praised Overton so warmly—how could I help it?—that she has decided to cast her lot there. Hence my telegram, also this letter. Please be as nice with her as you know how to be, for I am sure she will prove herself a credit to Overton.

"I shall hope to see you some time during the fall. I am going to try to get a day or two off and run down to see you. Tell Anne the Press is greater than the Stage, and tell Elfreda and Miriam that I am collecting the autographs of famous people and that theirs would be greatly appreciated, particularly if attached to letters. I must bring this epistle to an abrupt close, and go out on the trail of an engagement, the rumor of which was whispered to me last night. With love to you and the girls.

"MABEL.

"P. S. Frances sails for home next week."

"What a nice letter," commented Elfreda. "It is just like her, isn't it!"

"Yes," replied Grace slowly. "Girls, do you suppose Mabel and Miss West are really friends?"

"Not as we are," replied Miriam, with a positive shake of her head. "Elfreda and I were talking of that very thing while you were in your room. Elfreda said she didn't believe that Mabel had known Miss West long."

"What is the matter with us?" asked Grace, a trifle impatiently. "Here we are prowling about the bush, trying to conceal under polite inquiry the fact that we don't quite approve of Miss West. We would actually like to dig up something to criticize."

"There is nothing like absolute freedom of speech, is there?" said Elfreda, with a short laugh.

"It is true, though," said Grace stoutly. "It isn't fair, either. She has done nothing to deserve it. Besides, Mabel likes her."

"Mabel doesn't say in her letter that she likes her," reminded Anne. "She says Miss West is clever and that she admires her spirit."

"You, too, Anne?" said Grace reproachfully.

"I don't like her," declared Elfreda belligerently. "If it weren't for Mabel's letter I'd leave her strictly to her own devices."

"We ought to be ashamed of ourselves!" exclaimed Grace. "We have met Miss West with smiles, and here we are discussing her behind her back."

"I didn't meet her with smiles," contradicted Elfreda. "I was as sober as a judge all the time we stood talking to her. She is too flippant to suit me. She doesn't take college very seriously. I could see that."

"There goes the dinner bell!" exclaimed Grace, with sudden irrelevance to the subject of the newspaper girl. "Let us stop gossiping and go to dinner."

At dinner Grace was not sorry to note that Kathleen West had been placed at the end of the table farthest from her. Through the meal she found her eyes straying often toward the erect little figure of the newcomer, who, exhibiting not a particle of reserve, chatted with the girls nearest to her with the utmost unconcern. "I suppose her newspaper training has made her self-possessed and not afraid of strangers," reflected Grace. But she could not refrain from secretly wondering a little just how strong a friendship existed between Kathleen West and Mabel.

CHAPTER IV

GETTING ACQUAINTED WITH THE NEWSPAPER GIRL

"It was just this way," began Kathleen West, setting down her tea cup and looking impressively from one girl to the other, "Long before I graduated from high school I had made up my mind to go to college. Now that I have passed my exams and have become a really truly freshman, I'll tell you all about it."

Elfreda and Miriam were giving a tea party with Grace, Anne and Kathleen West as their guests. It was a strictly informal tea and both hostesses and guests sat on the floor in true Chinese fashion, kimono-clad and comfortable. A week had passed since Kathleen's advent among them. She had spent the greater part of that time either in study or in valiant wrestling with the dreaded entrance examinations, but she had managed, nevertheless, to drop into the girls' rooms at least once a day. In spite of the almost unfavorable impression she had at first created, it was impossible not to acknowledge that the newspaper girl possessed a vividly interesting personality. As she sat wrapped in the folds of her gray kimono, arms folded over her chest, she looked not unlike a feminine Napoleon. Elfreda's quick eyes traced the resemblance.

"You look for all the world like Napoleon," she observed bluntly.

"Thank you," returned Kathleen with mock gratitude. "I can't imagine Napoleon in a gray kimono at a tea party, but I feel imbued with a certain amount of his ambition. By the way, would any of you like to hear the rest of my story?" she asked impudently. "I'm rather fond of telling it."

"Excuse me for interrupting," apologized Elfreda. "Go on, please."

"Where was I?" asked Kathleen. "Oh, yes, I remember. Well, as soon as I had fully determined to go to college, I began to save every penny on which I could honestly lay hands. I went without most of the school-girl luxuries that count for so much just at that time. You girls know what I mean. Mother and Father didn't wish me to go to college. They planned a course in stenography and typewriting for me after I should finish high school, and when I pleaded for college they were angry and disappointed. They argued, too, that they couldn't possibly afford to send me there. As soon as I saw that I was going to have trouble with them, I kept my own counsel, but I was more determined than ever to do as I pleased. At the beginning of the vacation before my senior year in high school I went to the only daily paper in our town and asked for work. The editor, who had known me since I was a baby, gave me a chance. Father and Mother made no objection to that. They thought it was merely a whim on my part. But it wasn't a whim, as they found out later, for I wrote stuff for the paper during my senior year, too, and when I did graduate I turned the house upside down by getting a position on a newspaper in a big city. Father and Mother forgave me after awhile, but not until I had been at work on the other paper for a year.

"At first I did society, then clubs, went back to society again, and at last my opportunity came to do general reporting. I was the only woman on the staff who had a chance to go after the big stories. I have been doing that only the last two years, though.

"Naturally, I made more money on the paper than I would as a stenographer. I saved it, too. It was ever so much harder to hang on to it in the city. There were so many more ways to spend it. But I kept on putting it away, and, now, by going back on the paper every summer, I will have enough to see me through college."

"But why do you wish so much for a college education when you are already successful as a newspaper woman?" asked Elfreda.

"Because I want to be an author, or an editor, or somebody of importance in the literary world, and I need these four years at college. Besides, it's a good thing to bear the college stamp if one expects always to be before the public," was the prompt retort.

"Suppose you were to find afterward that you weren't going to be before the public," said Elfreda almost mischievously.

"But I shall be," persisted Kathleen, setting her jaws with a little snap. "I always accomplish whatever I set out to do. On the paper they used to say, 'Kathleen would sacrifice her best friend if by doing it she could scoop the other papers.'"

"What do you mean by 'scoop the other papers'?" queried Elfreda interestedly.

"Why, to get ahead of them with a story," explained Kathleen. "Suppose I found out an important piece of news that no one else knew. If I gave it to my paper and it appeared in it before any other newspaper got hold of it then that would be a scoop."

"Oh, yes, I see," returned Elfreda. "Then a scoop might be news about anything."

"Exactly," nodded Kathleen. "The harder the news is to get, the better story it makes. People won't tell one anything, and when one does find out something startling, then there are always a few persons who make a fuss and try to keep the story out of the paper. They generally have such splendid excuses for not wanting a story published. I never paid any attention to them, though. I turned in every story I ever ran down," she concluded, her small face setting in harsh lines.

"But didn't that make some of the people about whom the stories were written very unhappy?" asked Miriam pointedly.

"I suppose so," answered Kathleen. "But I never stopped to bother about them. I had to think of myself and of my paper."

"How long have you known Mabel Ashe?" asked Grace, abruptly changing the subject. Something in the cold indifference of Kathleen's voice jarred on her.

"Just since she appeared on the paper," returned Kathleen unconcernedly. "She is very pretty, isn't she? But prettiness alone doesn't count for much on a newspaper. Can she make good? That is the question. She imagines that journalism is her vocation, but I am afraid she is going to be sadly disillusioned. She seems to be a clever girl, though."

"Clever," repeated Grace with peculiar emphasis. "She is the cleverest girl we know. While she was at Overton, she was the life of the college. Everyone loved her. I can't begin to tell you how much we miss her."

"It's very nice to be missed, I am sure," said Kathleen hastily, retreating from what appeared to be dangerous ground. "I hope I shall be eulogized when I have graduated from Overton."

"That will depend largely on your behavior as a freshman," drawled Elfreda.

"What do you mean?" asked Kathleen sharply. "I thought freshmen were of the least importance in college."

"So they are to the other classes," returned Elfreda. "They are of the greatest importance to themselves, however, and if they make false starts during their freshman year it is likely to handicap them through the other three."

"Much obliged for the information," declared Kathleen flippantly. "I'll try not to make any false starts. Good gracious! It is half-past ten. I had no idea it was so late. I've had a lovely time at your tea party. I'm going to send out invitations for a social gathering before long." She rose lazily to her feet, and carefully set her cup on the table. "I suppose Miss Ainslee will be sound asleep," she remarked, yawning. "Lighting the gas will awaken her and she will be cross. She goes to bed with the chickens."

"Don't light it, then," suggested Grace. "You can see to undress with the blind up. There is full moon to-night."

"Why shouldn't I light it?" asked Kathleen. "Half of the room is mine. I wouldn't grumble if the case were reversed. She will soon grow used to the light. I intend occasionally to read or study after hours. Don't tell me it is against the rules. I know it. But circumstances, etc. I'll see you to-morrow. I wish I were a junior. The freshmen I have met so far are regular babies. I'm going to study hard next summer and see if I can't pass up the sophomore year. There is nothing like having a modest ambition, you know."

With this satirical comment the newspaper girl nodded a pert good night and left the room.

No one spoke after she had gone.

"I must go to bed," said Grace, breaking the significant silence that had fallen on the quartette. "Come, Anne, it's twenty minutes to eleven. Good night, girls."

"What do you think of Miss West, Anne?" asked Grace a little later as they were preparing to retire.

"I don't like to say," returned Anne slowly. "She's remarkably bright—" Anne paused. Her eyes met Grace's.

"I know," nodded Grace understandingly. "We will try to keep a starboard eye on her. She is going to find college very different from being a newspaper woman." Grace smiled faintly. The word "woman," as applied to Kathleen West, seemed wholly amusing.

"I don't think she showed particularly good taste in speaking as she did of Mabel Ashe," criticized Anne, a moment later. "I didn't intend to say that, but I might as well be perfectly frank with you, Grace."

"I was sorry she spoke as she did, too," agreed Grace. She did not add that the newspaper girl's half slighting remarks about Mabel Ashe still rankled in her loyal soul. It was chiefly to please Mabel that she and her friends had hospitably received this stranger into their midst, prepared to do whatever lay within their power to make her feel at home with them. And she had dared to speak almost disparagingly of the girl who was beloved by every student in Overton who knew her. In spite of her resolution to keep a "starboard eye" on the freshman, Grace felt infinitely more like leaving the ungrateful freshman to shift for herself.

"Well, what about her?" Elfreda asked bluntly of Miriam, as she piled the tea cups one inside the other.

"What about who?" returned Miriam tantalizingly.

"You know very well" declared Elfreda; "but, if I must be explicit, what do you think of Miss West now?"

"What do you think?" counter-questioned Miriam.

"I think she has more to learn than I had when I came here," said Elfreda speculatively, "and unless I am very much mistaken it will take her longer to learn it."

CHAPTER V

TWO IS A COMPANY

"Grace! Grace Harlowe!" called a clear, high voice. On hearing her name, Grace, who was on the point of entering the library, turned to greet Arline Thayer, who came running up the walk, flushed and laughing.

"Did you say you had won prizes as a champion fast walker?" she inquired laughingly. "I saw you clear across the campus, and I've been running at top speed ever since. I had just breath enough left to call to you. Where have you been hiding? I haven't seen you for ages. Ruth thinks you have deserted her. Don't bother going to the library now. Suppose we go down to Vinton's and have luncheon. Have you eaten yours? I never eat luncheon at Morton Hall on Saturday afternoon."

"I'll answer your questions in the order they were asked," laughed Grace. "No, I am not a champion fast walker. I haven't been hiding, and I still live at Wayne Hall, though a certain young person I know has evidently forgotten it. Ruth owes me a visit, and I haven't had my luncheon. You mustn't tempt me from my duty, for I am on the trail of knowledge. I must spend at least two hours this afternoon looking up a multitude of references."

"Come and have luncheon first and look up your references afterward," coaxed Arline. "Then, perhaps, I can help you," she added artfully.

"Perhaps you can," returned Grace dubiously. Their eyes meeting, both girls laughed.

"Come with me, at any rate, then," declared Arline.

"All right. Remember, I must not stay away from work over an hour. I really have a great deal to do. Isn't it a glorious day, though? Elfreda and Miriam went for a five-mile tramp. Elfreda is determined to play basketball in spite of her junior responsibilities, therefore she is obliged to train religiously."

"Who is going to play on the junior team this year?" asked Arline.

"Elizabeth Wade, and that little Tenbrook girl, Marian Cummings, Elfreda and Violet Darby make the team. Neither Miriam nor I intend to play. Elfreda begged hard, but we thought it better to stay out of the team this year. We have played basketball so long, and having been in two big games, it is time we resigned gracefully; besides, I want to see Elfreda reap the benefit of her faithful practice and distinguish herself. She has tried so hard to make the team."

"I am glad Elfreda is to have her chance," smiled Arline. "We are sure to see her make the most of it. I'm sorry now that I never went in for basketball."

"It is a wonderful old game!" exclaimed Grace with enthusiasm. "Last year was my sixth year on a team. I was captain of our freshman basketball team at home. That reminds me, Arline, aren't you and Ruth coming home with me for the Easter vacation? I am asking you early so no one else will have a chance. I know it is useless to ask you to come for Christmas."

"I think I can come for Easter," replied Arline, "and I don't know of any reason why Ruth can't. I shall write to Father at once and ask him if we can go. I want to tell you something, Grace—confidentially, of course. Father is very fond of Ruth. He and I had a talk this summer, and he wishes to adopt her. Just think of having Ruth for my very own sister!" Arline paused, her eyes shining.

Grace nodded understandingly. "What does Ruth say?" she asked.

Arline's face clouded. "She doesn't say anything except that she thinks it better for her to go on in her own way. She is the queerest girl. She seems to think that it wouldn't be right to allow Father to adopt her and take care of her. She says she has everything she needs now, and that I have been far too good to her. Father and I simply made her spend the summer with us."

Grace Harlowe's Third Year at Overton College

"Wouldn't it be wonderful if Ruth should find her father?" said Grace musingly.

"I don't believe she ever will," returned Arline. "It's too bad." Her flower-like face looked very solemn for a moment, then brightened as she exclaimed: "Oh, I almost forgot my principal reason for wishing to see you. The Semper Fidelis Club hasn't held a meeting this year, and we must begin to busy ourselves. I have heard of five different girls who need help, but are too proud to ask for it. I am sure there are dozens of others, too. We must find some way to reach and help them. We have plenty of money in our treasury now, and we can afford to be generous. Here we are at Vinton's. Shall we sit in the mission alcove for luncheon? I love it. It is so convenient when one wishes to indulge in strictly confidential conversation."

Once seated opposite each other in the cunning little alcove furnished in mission oak, Arline continued animatedly:

"Last spring, when we talked about giving an entertainment, you proposed giving a carnival in the fall. Well, it is fall now, so why not begin making plans for our carnival! What shall we have, and what do we do to draw a crowd?"

"We held a bazaar in Oakdale that was very successful," commented Grace. "We held it on Thanksgiving night and half the town attended it. We made over five hundred dollars. I think a bazaar would be better than a carnival." Grace did not add that the money had been stolen while the bazaar was at its height and not recovered until the following spring, by no other person than herself.

Those who have read "GRACE HARLOWE'S SENIOR YEAR AT HIGH SCHOOL" will remember the mysterious disappearance of the bazaar money and the untiring zeal with which Grace worked until she found a clew to the robbery, which led to the astonishing discovery that she made in an isolated house on the outskirts of Oakdale.

During the progress of the luncheon Grace gave Arline a detailed account of the various attractions of which their bazaar had boasted.

"We can ask some girl who sings to preside at the Shamrock booth and sing Irish songs as Nora O'Malley did," planned Grace. "We can't have the Mystery Auction, because we don't care to ask the girls for packages, and we can't have the Italian booth, either, it would be too hard to arrange, but we can have a gypsy camp and a Japanese booth and an English tea shop and two or three funny little shows. The best thing to do is to call a meeting of the club and put the matter before them. Almost every girl will know of some feature we can have."

"I suppose the dean will allow us to use the gymnasium," mused Arline. "We had better get permission first of all. Then we can call our meeting."

Grace looked at her watch. "I've stayed ten minutes over my hour, Arline," she reminded the little curly-haired girl.

"Never mind," was the calm reply, "you can stay ten minutes longer in the library. Oh, Grace, don't look at her now, but who is that girl just sitting down at that end table? I am sure she lives at Wayne Hall. Some one told me she was a freshman."

"If you had been calling faithfully on the Wayne Hall girls, you wouldn't need to be told the names of the new ones," flung back Grace. Then, allowing her gaze to slowly travel about the room, her eyes rested as though by chance on the girl designated by Arline. An instant later she had bowed to the newcomer in friendly fashion.

"Who is she?" murmured Arline, her eyes fixed upon Grace.

"Her name is Kathleen West," returned Grace in a low tone. "Don't say anything more. Here she comes."

Kathleen was approaching their table, a bored look on her small, sharp face. "How are you?" she said nonchalantly. "I thought I'd come over here. Having tea alone is dull. Don't you think so?"

Arline's blue eyes rested on the intruder for the fraction of a second. She resented the intrusion.

"Miss West, this is Miss Thayer, of the junior class," introduced Grace good-naturedly. Both girls bowed. There was an awkward silence, broken by Kathleen's abrupt, "I knew I had seen you before, Miss Thayer," to Arline.

"That is quite possible," said Arline, rather stiffly. "I believe I remember passing you on the campus."

"Oh, I don't mean here at Overton," drawled Kathleen. "I saw you in New York with your father last summer."

"With my father?" was Arline's surprised interrogation.

"Yes. Isn't Leonard B. Thayer your father?"

"Why, how did you know? Have you met my father?" Arline's blue eyes opened wider.

"I've seen him," said Kathleen laconically. "I tried to interview him once, but couldn't get past his secretary."

"Miss West is a newspaper woman, Arline," explained Grace. "That is, she was one. She has deserted her paper for Overton, however."

"How interesting," responded Arline courteously. "Do you like college, Miss West?"

"Fairly well," answered Kathleen. "It doesn't really matter whether I like it or not. I am here for business, not pleasure. Perhaps Miss Harlowe has told you how I happened to be here."

"Miss Thayer and I had some weighty class matters to discuss," said Grace, smiling a little. "We weren't talking of any one in particular. Miss Thayer did inquire your name when she saw me bow to you. I answered just as you came toward us," added Grace honestly.

"I knew you were talking about me," declared Kathleen flippantly. "One can always feel when one is being discussed."

A quick flush rose to Grace's cheeks. Usually tolerant toward everyone, she felt a decided resentment stir within her at this cold-blooded assertion that she and Arline had been gossiping.

Arline's blue eyes sent forth a distinctly hostile glance. "You were mistaken, Miss West," she said coldly. "What was said of you was entirely impersonal."

"Oh, I don't doubt that in the least," Kathleen hastened to say. She had decided that the daughter of Leonard B. Thayer was worth cultivating. "I am sorry you misunderstood me; but do you know, when you made that last remark you looked as your father did the day he wouldn't tell me a thing I wanted to know." Kathleen's sharp features were alive with the interest of discovery.

Despite their brief annoyance Grace and Arline both laughed. Kathleen took instant advantage of the situation. "Suppose we order another pot of tea," she said hospitably.

It was fully half an hour later when the three girls left Vinton's.

"Oh, my neglected references," sighed Grace. "I must not lose another minute of the afternoon. Which way are you girls going?"

"I think I'll go as far as the library with you, Grace," decided Arline. The interruption by Kathleen had greatly interfered with her plans.

"I might as well go with you," remarked Kathleen innocently. "I have nothing to do this afternoon."

A little frown wrinkled Arline's smooth forehead. Grace, equally disappointed, managed to conceal her annoyance. Then, accepting the situation in the best possible spirit, she slipped her hand through Arline's arm, at the same time giving it a warning pressure. During the walk to the library Kathleen endeavored to make herself particularly agreeable to Arline, a method of procedure that was not lost upon Grace. Later as she delved industriously among half a dozen dignified volumes for the material of which she stood in need, Kathleen's pale, sharp face, with its thin lips and alert eyes, rose before her, and, for the first time, she admitted reluctantly to herself that her dislike for the ambitious little newspaper girl was very real indeed.

CHAPTER VI

AN UNSUSPECTED LISTENER

"Those in favor of giving a bazaar on the Saturday afternoon and evening of November fifteenth say 'aye,'" directed Arline Thayer.

A chorus of ayes immediately resounded.

"Contrary, 'no,'" continued Arline.

There was a dead silence.

"Carried," declared the energetic little president. "Please, everyone think hard and try to advance an idea for a feature inside of the next ten minutes."

The twelve young women known as the Semper Fidelis Club were holding a business meeting in Grace Harlowe's and Anne Pierson's, room. The two couch beds had been placed in a kind of semicircle and eight members of the club were seated on them. The other three young women sat on cushions on the floor, while Arline presided at the center table, which had been placed several feet in front of the members.

"The meeting is open for suggestions," repeated Arline after two minutes had elapsed and not a word had been said. "If any one has a suggestion, she may tell us without addressing the chair. We will dispense with formality," she added encouragingly. "Of course, we know we are going to have the gypsy encampment and the Irish booth and the Japanese tea room, but we want some really startling features."

"We might have an 'Alice in Wonderland' booth," suggested Elfreda. "'Alice' stunts always go in colleges. The girls are never tired of them."

"What on earth is an 'Alice in Wonderland booth'?" asked Gertrude Wells curiously.

"I don't know what it is yet," grinned Elfreda. "The idea just came to me. I suppose," she continued reflectively, "we could have all the animals, like the March Hare, for instance, and the Dormouse. Then there's the Mock Turtle and the Jabberwock. No, that's been done to death. Besides, it's in 'Through the Looking Glass.' We could have the Griffon, though, and then, there's the Duchess, the King, the Queen, and the Mad Hatter. I'd love to do the Mad Hatter." Elfreda paused, eyeing the little group quizzically.

"I think that's a brilliant idea, Elfreda!" exclaimed Grace warmly.

"Great!" exulted three or four girls, in lively chorus.

"I'll tell you what we could have," cried one of the Emerson twins. "Why not make it an 'Alice in Wonderland Circus,' and have all the animals perform?"

"We are growing more brilliant with every minute," laughed Arline. "That is a positive inspiration, Sara."

"A circus will exactly fill the bill. It is sure to be the biggest feature the Overton girls have ever spent their money to see," predicted Elfreda gleefully. "Ruth Denton, you will have to be the Dormouse."

"Oh, I can't," blushed Ruth.

"Oh, you can," mimicked Elfreda. "I'll help you plan your costume."

"Will the club please come to order," called Arline, for a general buzz of conversation had begun. "We shall have to choose part of our animals from outside the club. We can't all be in the circus. Grace and Miriam are going to dress as gypsies. Julia and Sara," smiling at the black-eyed twins, who looked precisely alike and were continually being mistaken for each other, "are going to be Japanese ladies, aren't you, girls?"

The twins nodded emphatically.

"Those in favor of an Alice in Wonderland Circus please say 'aye,'" dutifully stated Arline. The motion was quickly carried. "That is only one feature," she reminded. "This meeting is open for further suggestions. Let us have the suggestions first, then we can discuss them in detail afterward."

After considerable hard thinking, a "bauble shop," a postcard booth, and a doll shop were added. The latter idea was Ruth Denton's. "Now that it is fall, Christmas isn't so very far off. Almost every girl has a little sister or a niece or a friend to whom she intends to give a doll," she said almost wistfully. "We could pledge ourselves to contribute one doll at least, and as many more as we please. Then we could draw on the treasury for a certain sum and invest it in dolls. We could dress a few of them as college girls, too. I'm willing to use part of my spare time to help the good work along. Perhaps it wouldn't be a success," she faltered.

"Success!" exclaimed Arline, stumbling over Gertrude Wells's feet and treating Ruth to an affectionate hug. "I think it's perfectly lovely. We can have a live doll, too. Do any of you know that exquisite little freshman with the big blue eyes who rooms at Mortimer Hall?"

"I do. Her name is Myra Stone," responded Julia Emerson. "She looks like a big doll, doesn't she!"

"She does," commented Arline. "That is precisely what I was thinking. Dressed as a live doll and placed on exhibition in the middle of the booth, she would prove a drawing card. Will you ask her to meet us at the gymnasium on Monday at five o'clock? We will try to see the others we want for the bazaar before Monday. We had better decide now just who is going to be left over for the circus."

"There is only one objection to little Miss Stone," said Gertrude Wells thoughtfully. "She is a freshman. I am afraid this mark of upper class favor may cause jealousy."

"The freshmen ought to be glad one of their class is to have the honor of being chosen," retorted Grace, opening her gray eyes in surprise.

"They ought to, but they won't be," predicted Gertrude dryly. "There are a number of revolutionary spirits among the freshmen this year. That queer little West girl, who styles herself a 'newspaper woman' and looks like a wicked little elf, is the ringleader."

"She is very bright, Gertrude, and she deserves a great deal of credit for the way she has worked and studied to fit herself for college," defended Grace, her old love of fair play coming to the surface.

"That may all be so. I believe it is, if you say so, Grace, but why doesn't she display common sense enough to settle down and obey the rules of the college? She doesn't transgress the study rules, but she is lawless when it comes to the others. Besides, she runs roughshod over traditions, and all that they imply. She—well—" Gertrude hesitated, then, flushing slightly, stopped.

"You mean she is tricky, don't you?" asked Elfreda promptly. "I could see that before I talked with her five minutes."

Grace shook her head disapprovingly at Elfreda. Something in her glance caused Elfreda to subside suddenly.

"If there is no further business of which to dispose, will some one make a motion that we adjourn!" asked Arline quietly.

The motion was made and seconded, but before any one had time to step into the hall, a slight figure flitted from her position before the almost closed door, and disappeared into the room at the end of the hall.

"We must be sure and see the dean as soon as we can, Arline," called Grace after Arline, who was hurrying down the hall to overtake Ruth.

"I'll see her to-morrow afternoon," assured Arline, with a parting wave of her hand as she disappeared down the stairs.

"And I'll make it my business to see her to-morrow morning," muttered Kathleen West vindictively, who, standing well within the shadow of her own door at the end of the hall, had heard the remark and the reply. "Who knows but that the Semper Fidelis Club may not be able to give their great bazaar after all. They certainly won't if I can prevent them. I'll never forgive them for discussing me as they have this afternoon." There was an unpleasant light in the newspaper girl's eyes, as, closing the door of her room, she went to her desk and opening it, sat down before it, picking up her pen.

After a little thought she began to write, and when she had finished what seemed to be an extremely short letter, she slipped it into the envelope with a smile of malicious satisfaction. She had found a way to retaliate.

CHAPTER VII

AN UNPLEASANT SUMMONS

"Here's a letter for you, Grace," called Elfreda, who had run downstairs ahead of Grace to survey the contents of the house bulletin board before going in to breakfast.

Grace surveyed the envelope critically, tore it open and unfolded the sheet of paper inside. In another moment a little cry of consternation escaped her.

"What's the matter?" asked Elfreda curiously, trying to peer over her shoulder.

"It—it's a summons from the dean," said Grace a trifle unsteadily. "What do you suppose it means?"

"Nothing very serious," declared Elfreda confidently. "How can it? Think over your past misdeeds and see if you can discover any reason for a summons."

Grace shook her head. "No," she said slowly. "I can't think of a single, solitary thing."

"Then don't worry about it," was Elfreda's comforting advice. "Whatever it is, you are ready for it."

As Grace entered the dean's office that morning a vague feeling of apprehension rose within her. The dean, a stately, dark-haired woman with a rather forbidding expression, which disappeared the moment she smiled, glanced up with a flash of approval at the fine, resolute face of the gray-eyed girl who walked straight to her and said firmly, "Good morning, Miss Wilder."

"Good morning, Miss Harlowe," returned the dean quietly. Then picking up a letter that lay on the middle of her desk, she said gravely: "I received a very peculiar letter this morning, Miss Harlowe, and as it concerns not only you, but a number of your friends as well, I thought it better to send for you. You may throw light upon what at present seems obscure."

Grace mechanically stretched forth her hand for the open letter and read: —

> "When giving an entertainment in any of the halls or in the gymnasium, is it not usually customary, not to say courteous, to ask permission of the president of the college or the dean beforehand? The young women whose names appear on the enclosed list evidently do not consider any such permission necessary. For the past week preparations for a bazaar have been going briskly forward, to be held in the gymnasium on the evening of November — —. For inside information inquire of Miss Harlowe.
>
> "A Well Wisher."

Grace read the note through twice, then, looking squarely at the dean, she said: "May I see the enclosed list?" The dean handed her a smaller slip of paper on which appeared the names of the girls who had been present at the meeting in her room. Grace scanned the slip earnestly. Her color rose slightly as she returned it to Miss Wilder.

"The names on this list are the names of the young women who belong to the Semper Fidelis Club. After the concert last spring it was partly decided to give a bazaar the following autumn. The other day the club met in my room to talk over the matter. As we were all in favor of giving one, the meeting was open for the discussion of ideas for attractive features. Finally something was proposed that was so very clever we couldn't help adopting it. I assure you, Miss Wilder, we had no thought of doing anything definite about the bazaar without first obtaining proper permission to give it and to use the gymnasium as our field of operation. In fact, Miss Thayer promised me on the afternoon of the meeting that she would see you the following afternoon. She is the president of the club. I haven't seen her since then." Grace paused, looking worried.

"Miss Thayer has not been here," returned Miss Wilder kindly. "However, your explanation is sufficient, Miss Harlowe. I am reasonably sure that the writer of this letter has either misunderstood the situation, or has been misinformed. To be candid, very little credence can be placed on the information contained in an anonymous letter. In fact, my reason for sending for you had to do with that, rather than the implied charge the letter makes. I wish you to examine this handwriting," she touched the letter which Grace still held in hand. "Do you recognize it?"

There was a slight interval of silence. Grace devoted herself to the examination of the letter and the slip of paper. Then, handing it to the dean, she said frankly: "I have no recollection of having seen this handwriting before to-day."

The dean folded the letter, placed the list of names inside its folds and returned it to the envelope. "This is the first anonymous letter that has ever been brought to my notice," she said gravely. "I trust it will be the last. It is hard to believe that a student of Overton would resort to such petty spite, for that seems to be its keynote. It is practically impossible, however, to find the writer among so many girls."

Grace would have liked to say that this was not the first anonymous letter that had been brought to her notice. The ghost of a disturbing, unsigned note that had almost wrecked Elfreda's freshman happiness rose and walked before her. Could it be possible that the same hand had written the second note? Grace was startled at her own thought.

"May I see the note again, Miss Wilder?" she asked soberly. This time she scrutinized the writing even more closely. There was something familiar, yet unfamiliar, about the formation of the letters. Finally she handed it back. "It is a mystery to me," she said, with a little sigh. "I am so glad you understood about the bazaar."

Before the dean could reply the click of approaching heels was heard. A moment later a light knock sounded on the door. At a nod from the dean, Grace opened it, and stood face to face with Arline Thayer.

"Why, Grace Harlowe!" she exclaimed in her sweet, high voice. "I didn't know you were here. Did you get my message? Good afternoon, Miss Wilder," she added, following Grace inside the office.

"Good afternoon, Miss Thayer," smiled Miss Wilder, indicating a chair, which Arline accepted.

"I owe you and the Semper Fidelis Club an apology for not having delivered their message. I spent yesterday nursing a headache and was not able to attend any of my classes. Miss Harlowe has already asked your permission to hold a bazaar in the gymnasium, I believe."

"Yes," returned Miss Wilder pleasantly. "I am willing to allow the Semper Fidelis Club carte blanche for one night. I approve warmly of both the club and its object. I shall, of course, ask formal permission of the president, but that need not necessarily delay your plans. The concert given by your club last year was a most enjoyable affair and proved very profitable to the club, did it not?"

Grace answered in the affirmative. "We were fortunate in being able to secure Savelli, the virtuoso," she replied. "It was by the merest chance that he happened to have that one evening free. His daughter, Eleanor, who is one of my dear friends, and I telephoned to New York City to ask him to play for us. We saved him until last as a surprise number."

"The audience fully appreciated his playing," returned Miss Wilder. "To hear the great Savelli was an unexpected privilege. I shall look forward to your bazaar with pleasurable anticipation and I wish you success."

Grace looked searchingly into the smiling, dark eyes of the dean.

"Thank you so much, Miss Wilder," she said earnestly. "I felt sure you would understand."

"We should like Professor Morton to open the bazaar, and would appreciate a speech from you also," added Arline.

"I shall be pleased to help the club in any way I can," assured Miss Wilder graciously as the two girls were about to leave the office. "I am certain that Professor Morton will echo my sentiments." Something in the older woman's quiet tones made Grace feel that the anonymous letter had entirely failed in its object.

CHAPTER VIII

ELFREDA PROPHESIES TROUBLE

Not until the two girls were well outside did either venture to speak. Then their eyes met. "Did you receive my message?" asked Arline abruptly.

"Your message," repeated Grace. "No, I didn't receive any message. By whom did you send it?"

"Emma Dean," declared Arline. "She was at Morton House yesterday for luncheon, and I ran across her in the hall. I asked her to ask you if you would see Miss Wilder after classes yesterday afternoon."

"Emma Dean again," laughed Grace. "Didn't you know, Arline, that the Dean messenger service is absolutely unreliable? Emma is always perfectly willing to deliver a message, but never remembers to deliver it. Only last week Elfreda made an engagement with a dressmaker who sews for Emma. In the meantime Emma went to the dressmaker's house for a fitting, and the woman asked her to tell Elfreda to come for her fitting on Thursday instead of Friday night. Emma forgot it before she was a block from the dressmaker's, and poor Elfreda dutifully trudged off to her fitting instead of accepting an invitation to a theatre party that the girls got up on Friday afternoon. The dressmaker wasn't in and Elfreda went home angry. Emma delivered the message the next day."

"No wonder you didn't receive mine then," laughed Arline.

"How did you happen to find me?" asked Grace.

"Oh, I wasn't looking for you," replied Arline. "I thought as long as I felt better, I had better call on Miss Wilder, too. But," said Arline, a puzzled look creeping into her eyes, "if you didn't receive my message, how did you happen to be in the dean's office?"

"I received a summons," answered Grace quietly. "The dean wished to see me about—well—" Grace hesitated. "I should like to tell you about it," she went on. "Miss Wilder did not ask me to keep the matter a secret. That was understood, I suppose. But, Arline, I think it would be better to ask her permission before telling even you."

"Is it anything about me or about the club?" asked Arline curiously.

"It is something about the club," replied Grace enigmatically.

"Then suppose we go back and ask her now," proposed Arline.

"No," negatived Grace wisely, "it wouldn't do. Wait a little. I shall see her again in a day or two. Then I may have a chance to ask her."

"All right," sighed Arline disappointedly. "Now that we have permission we must go to work with a will. The 'Circus' must meet and plan the costumes. Each girl will have to furnish her own. Ruth said she thought she could design them all, and cut them out if the girls could do their own sewing."

"Ruth is doing too much," demurred Grace. "Remember she is going to help dress dolls for the doll shop."

"I know it," responded Arline, "but, thanks to the Semper Fidelis Club, she doesn't have to burden herself with mending. Besides, I keep her so busy with my clothes she doesn't have time to do anything for outsiders. Some of the girls were so provoking. They used to give her their work at the eleventh hour, and then send for it before she had half a chance to finish it. They didn't exert themselves to pay her, however. It was weeks, sometimes, before they gave her the money. They usually forgot about it and spent their allowance money for something else. I think I have already told you that Father would adopt Ruth if she would consent to it. But she is a most stiff-necked young person. She says she must work out her own salvation, and that too much comfort might spoil her for doing good work in the world."

"Do you suppose her father is really dead?" asked Grace thoughtfully.

"Oh, I think he must be," returned Arline quickly. "Even if he isn't dead, there is only one chance in a thousand of her finding him.

When I went home last June I had one of my famous talks with Father. We decided that I needed a competent person to look after me in college, and Father asked Ruth to accept the position of companion. Then she could room with me and be free from this hateful sewing. But she wouldn't do it, the proud little thing! I like her all the better for her pride, though," concluded Arline in a burst of confidence.

"I think she is right about making her own way," declared Grace. "If I were placed in her circumstances I imagine I should look at the matter in the same light. Really, Arline, I often think that girls as happily situated as you and I do not half appreciate our benefits."

"I know it," agreed Arline. "Still, I am wide awake to the fact that a single room, pretty clothes and a generous allowance are not to be despised. I have grown so used to my way of living that to adopt Ruth's wouldn't be easy. I'd be worse off than she, for I don't know how to mend or sew or do anything else that is useful. I wonder if the girls would like me as well poor as rich," she said almost wistfully.

"Goose!" scoffed Grace. "Of course they would. How could any one help liking you? To change the subject, when shall we call a meeting of the bazaar specialists? We might as well post a notice on the big bulletin board. It will do more to advertise the bazaar than anything else."

"Grace, you are a born advertiser," cried Arline. "There will be a crowd around that bulletin board all day. Will you write the notice to-night? Oh, did I tell you? I'm going to have my horse here this year. Father wants me to ride."

"How lovely!" exclaimed Grace with a little sigh. "How I wish I had a horse. I'd willingly use all my allowance to feed one, if Father could afford to buy him for me."

"Mabel Ashe has the handsomest horse I ever saw," said Arline. "He is black as jet. You know I often see her in New York during vacations. We have ridden together several times."

"You mean Elixir," returned Grace. "I have never seen him, but I have heard of him. That reminds me, Mabel is coming down here for Thanksgiving. I received a letter from her yesterday."

"I wish she could come down for the bazaar," sighed Arline regretfully.

"So do I," responded Grace heartily.

At the corner above Wayne Hall Arline left Grace with a warning, "Don't forget to post that notice." As Grace reached the steps of the Hall the front door opened and two girls stepped out on the porch, followed by an alert little figure whose small face wore an expression of malicious amusement. "Do come again," she was saying in clear, high tones. "I've heard some very interesting things this afternoon." Looking down, simultaneously, three pairs of eyes were leveled on Grace and conversation instantly ceased. Grace walked quietly up the steps and, with a courteous "good afternoon," passed into the house and up the stairs to her room. Her face was unusually sober as she slowly pulled the hatpins from her hat. "How did Miss West happen to meet them?" she said half aloud.

"Meet whom?" asked Elfreda, who had come into the room in time to hear Grace's half musing question.

"Oh, Elfreda. How you startled me!" exclaimed Grace.

"How did Miss West meet whom? That's what I am curious to know," returned Elfreda, regarding Grace with lively interest.

"Alberta Wicks and Mary Hampton, Inquisitive," answered Grace.

"Where did you see them?" asked Elfreda, exhibiting considerable excitement.

"On the front porch. They had evidently been making a call on Kathleen."

"Then look out," predicted Elfreda. "They began back in the freshman year with me. Last year it was Laura Atkins and Mildred Taylor. This year it will be Kathleen West, and you mark my word, she won't reform at the end of the year as the rest of us did."

"'Quoth the raven, "nevermore",'" laughed Grace.

"Well, you'll see," declared Elfreda gloomily. "I'm sorry Kathleen West lives here. I thought we were going to have a peaceful year. But every fall apparently brings its problem. Really, Grace, I can't help feeling terribly remorseful to think that it is I who have caused all this trouble. If I hadn't been such an idiot when I first came here, you and Alberta Wicks and Mary Hampton might at least be on speaking terms."

"You mustn't think about such ancient history, Elfreda," admonished Grace. "We all do things for which we are afterward sorry. I daresay I should have offended those two girls in some other way before my freshman year was over. Both sides were to blame. I suppose we were naturally antagonistic."

"That is one way of putting it," muttered Elfreda, scowling over her past misdeeds.

"Come, come, Elfreda, don't glower over what has been forgotten," smiled Grace, patting Elfreda's plump shoulder.

"You may forget," declared the stout girl solemnly, "but I never shall."

CHAPTER IX

OPENING THE BAZAAR

It was Saturday afternoon, and the Semper Fidelis bazaar had just been opened. Grace Harlowe, attired in her gypsy costume, for which she had sent home, stood watching the gay scene, her eyes glowing with interest and pleasure. Professor Morton, the president of the college, had set his seal of approval on the bazaar by making a short speech. Then the dean had added a word or two, and the applause had died away in a pleasant hum of conversation that arose from the throng of students and visitors that more than comfortably filled the gymnasium.

"I don't see how those girls managed to accomplish so much in so short a time," remarked the dean to Miss Duncan. "I understand Miss Harlowe was a prime mover in the work."

"Yes," replied Miss Duncan. "Miss Harlowe seems to have plenty of initiative. She is one of the most active members of this new club, who have taken upon themselves the responsibility of helping needy students through college. I understand their treasury is already in a flourishing condition, thanks to their own efforts and a timely contribution they received after their concert last spring. I consider Miss Harlowe the finest type of young woman I have encountered during all my years of teaching," replied Miss Duncan warmly, which was a remarkable statement from this rather austere teacher.

"The junior class is particularly rich in good material," replied the dean. "I could name at least a dozen young women whom I consider splendid types of the ideal Overton girl."

Utterly unaware of the approval of the faculty, Grace had paused for a moment outside the gypsy encampment to cast a speculative eye over the crowd, which seemed to be steadily increasing.

"It is a brilliant success," she said to Arline gleefully, who had come up and now stood beside her. "I am so glad, but so tired. I do hope everyone will like the bazaar, and have a good time this afternoon and to-night. Everything has gone so beautifully. There hasn't been a sign of a hitch. Oh, yes, there was one." Her face clouded for a second. Then she looked at Arline brightly. "I'm not going to think of it. There are so many nice things to remember that one little unpleasantness doesn't count, does it?"

"I think it counts," declared Arline stubbornly. "I shall never forget it as long as I live. Why, it nearly spoiled our bazaar. It was dreadful to have some one spread the story of our circus, and just what we intended to have, when we wanted the whole thing to be a surprise."

"Really, I think the person who told the tales did us a good turn after all," laughed Grace. "The girls were ever so much more anxious to attend the bazaar after they heard of the circus. Every girl loves 'Alice in Wonderland,' I think. And then the Sphinx is a first-class surprise."

"Isn't it funny?" chuckled Arline, who, in her short, white, embroidered dress, pale blue sash, blue silk stockings and heelless blue kid slippers, her golden hair hanging in curls, tied up on one side with a blue ribbon, looked exactly as Lewis Carroll's immortal Alice might have looked if she had been inspired with life.

"Alice" was allowed to show herself to the public before the performance, and on catching sight of Grace had run across the gymnasium to her in true little girl fashion.

Never before had Overton's big gymnasium been so peculiarly and gayly arrayed. At one end a numerous band of gypsies had pitched their tents and here Grace and Miriam, garbed in the many-colored raiment of the Zingari, jingled their tambourines in their familiar but ever-popular Spanish dance, and read curious pink palms itching to know the future.

Adjoining the gypsy encampment was a doll shop, over which the cunning freshman, Myra Stone, dressed as a sailor doll, presided. Then came the Japanese tea shop, with the Emerson twins as proprietors, looking so realistically Japanese that Arline declared she didn't believe they were the Emerson twins, but two geisha girls straight from Japan. At intervals, when their patrons had all been served, they sidled up to the center of the shop and performed a quaint Oriental dance for the entertainment of their guests.

The Emerson Twins Looked Realistically Japanese.

Violet Darby had been asked to preside at the Shamrock booth instead of Arline, as had first been suggested, Arline having been elected to portray the world-renowned Alice. As an Irish colleen, Violet, however, proved a distinct success, and thrilled her hearers with "Kathleen Mavourneen" and "The Harp that Once Through Tara's Halls." Her voice held that peculiarly sweet, plaintive quality so necessary to bring out the beauty of the old Irish melodies, and Grace and Anne both agreed that there was only one who could surpass her. There was only one Nora O'Malley.

Farther on four pretty sophomores, dressed as Norman peasant girls, were dispensing cakes and ices to a steadily increasing patronage. There was a postcard and souvenir booth, around which a crowd seemed perpetually stationed. The souvenirs consisted mainly of small black and white or water color sketches contributed by the artistic element of Overton.

Occupying one entire end of the room was the circus ring, and on this public attention was centered. A gayly decorated poster at the door bore the pleasing information that there would be four performances, at two-thirty, four-thirty, eight-thirty, and nine-thirty, respectively, in which would appear the "Celebrated Alice in Wonderland Animals."

The club had originally planned to keep the matter of the circus as a surprise until the patrons of the bazaar should enter the gymnasium, but in some mysterious manner the secret had leaked out. Even the identity of certain animals was known, and when this unpleasant news had reached the ears of the "animals" themselves a meeting was called, which almost put an end to the circus then and there. After due consideration the performers agreed to go on with the spectacle, but many and indignant were the theories advanced as to the manner in which the news had traveled abroad. That the information had gone forth through a member of the club or any one taking part in the circus no one of them believed. Complete ostracism threatened the offender or offenders provided she or they, as the case might be, were discovered. Later the members of the club were forced to admit that, although the principle of the act was reprehensible, the act itself had served only as a means of advertising, and had aroused the curiosity and interest of the public.

After several earnest discussions on the part of the club, the admission fee had been fixed at twenty-five cents, and the public had been invited. As a college town Overton's "public" was largely made up of the classes rather than the masses, and many of the visitors claimed Overton as their Alma Mater. The students, however, were the hope on which the club based its dreams of profit. "No girl could walk around the gymnasium without spending money. She couldn't resist those darling shops. They are all too fascinating for words," Arline had declared rapturously as she and Grace were taking a last walk around the great, gayly decorated room before going to luncheon that day.

Now, as they stood side by side anxiously watching the steadily increasing tide of visitors, they agreed that their efforts were about to be rewarded.

"Isn't it splendid!" exulted Arline. "And, oh, have you seen the Sphinx, and isn't she great! How did Emma happen to think of her, let alone getting her up?"

"S-h-h!" cautioned Grace in a warning tone. "Some one might hear you."

"Oh, I forgot. Sphinxes are supposed to be shrouded in mystery, aren't they?"

"This one is," smiled Grace. Then her face sobered instantly. "I hope no one else besides ourselves finds out. We ought to keep her identity a secret. I think the idea is simply great, don't you?"

Arline nodded. "Come on over and see her," she coaxed.

A moment later they stood before the entrance to a small tent, hung with a heavy curtain. Pushing the curtain aside, Arline stepped into the tent. A burnoosed, turbaned Arab standing inside salaamed profoundly. The two girls giggled, and there was a stifled, most un-Arab-like echo from the bronzed son of the desert. Then they paused before a platform about four feet in height on which reposed what appeared to be a gigantic Sphinx, her paws stiffly folded in front of her.

"Ask me a question." This sudden, mysterious croak that issued from inside the great head caused Arline to start and step back. "Ask me a question. I am as old as the world. I am the world's great riddle, the one which has never been solved. Ask me a question, only one, one only." The eerie voice died away into yards of drapery that extended in huge folds from the back of the head and far out on the platform.

"How on earth did you ever get into that affair, and who made it?" asked Arline curiously.

"Mystery, all is mystery," croaked the Sphinx.

"But you said you would answer my question!" persisted Arline.

"Which one?" plaintively inquired the voice.

"Both," declared Arline boldly.

"Only one, only one," was the provoking reply.

"Then, who made it?" asked Arline.

"It was made ages ago." Emma Dean's familiar drawl startled both Grace and Arline. "My brother had it made for a college play called 'Sphinx.' When we began to plan for the bazaar I sent home for it. I was so afraid it wouldn't arrive on time. My brother hired an old man who does this wonderful papier mache work to make it. I made the paws. Rather realistic, aren't they? All this drapery came with the head. I am inside the head, sitting on a stool. It's rather dark and stuffy, but it's lots of fun, too. I can appear before the audience at any moment. The head is built over a light frame. There is an arrangement inside the head that makes promenading possible. In fact, I had practiced an attractive little dance—"

"Hurrah!" cried Arline. "Another feature. When shall we have it! Won't that be splendid?"

"Not this afternoon. Late in the evening," counseled Emma. "I don't wish to dance more than once, and you know what a college girl audience means. Now, is there anything else you want to know?"

There was a sudden murmur of voices outside which silenced Emma immediately. Then Alberta Wicks, Mary Hampton and Kathleen West were ushered into the tent.

"I am the Sphinx," began the far-away voice again in the mammoth head. "Ask me a question."

Bowing to the newcomers rather coldly, Grace and Arline turned to leave the tent. But Grace reflected grimly as she lifted the tent flap that if any one of the trio had been the all-wise Sphinx, instead of her friend Emma Dean, there were several questions she might have asked that would have been disconcerting to say the least.

A little later she strolled back to the Sphinx's tent, only to find that amiable riddle besieged by an impatient throng of girls who were eager to spend their money for the mere sake of hearing the Sphinx's ridiculous answers to their questions, and incidentally to try if possible to discover her identity. Emma had succeeded in changing her voice so completely that the far-away, almost wailing tones of the Egyptian wonder had little in common with her usual drawl. She and her faithful Arab had thoroughly enjoyed the attempts of the various girls to discover who was inside the great head and voluminous drapery.

"I would never have known who was in there if Emma herself had not told me. I don't believe any one outside the club knows either," was Grace's conclusion as she returned to her own booth. But in this she was mistaken.

CHAPTER X

THE ALICE IN WONDERLAND CIRCUS

The Alice in Wonderland Circus went down in the annals of Overton as the most original "stunt" ever attempted by any particular class. 19— bore its honors modestly, but was inordinately proud of the achievement of the Semper Fidelis Club.

The animals' costumes had been designed by Ruth and Elfreda. After much poring over half a dozen editions of "Alice," the original illustrations by "John Tenniel" had appealed most strongly to them, and these had been copied as faithfully as possible in style and color. The only important dry goods store in Overton had been ransacked for colored cambrics, denim and khaki, and under the clever fingers of Ruth, who seemed to know the exact shape and proportion of every one of the Wonderland "animals," the Dormouse, the Griffon and the Rabbit had been fitted with "skins." Elfreda had skilfully designed and made the Mock Turtle's huge shell and flappers, the Griffon's wings, not to mention ears for at least half the circus, and Gertrude Wells, whose clever posters were always in demand, obligingly painted bars, dots, stripes or whatever touch was needed to make the particular animal a triumph of realism. The King and Queen looked as though they might have stepped from the pages of the book, and the Duchess, as played by Anne, was a masterpiece of acting.

The circus opened with a grand march of the animals. Then followed the "Mad Hatter Quadrille," called by the Mad Hatter and danced by the March Hare, the Dormouse, the Rabbit, the Griffon, the Mock Turtle, the Dodo, the Duchess and Alice. Then the Mad Hatter stepped to the center of the ring, flourished his high hat, bowed profoundly, and made a funny little speech about the accomplishments of the animals, each one walking solemnly into the middle of the ring as his name was called and clumsily saluting the audience.

Then the real circus began. The Dormouse skipped the rope, the Rabbit balanced a plate on his nose, the Griffon, with a great flapping of wings, laboriously climbed a ladder and jumped from the top rung to the ground, a matter of about six feet, where he bowed pompously and waved his long claws to the audience. Then the Mock Turtle sang "Beautiful Soup," and wept so profusely he toppled over at the end of the song and lay flopping on his back. The Mad Hatter and the Griffon hastily raised him only to find he had made a dreadful dent in his shell. This did not hinder him from joining his friend, the Griffon, in "Won't You Join the Dance?" which stately caper they performed around Alice, while the other animals stood in a circle and marked time with their feet, solemnly waving their paws and wagging their heads in unison.

The Cheshire Cat, who had a real Chessy Cat head which Gertrude Wells had manufactured and painted, and who wore Arline's long squirrel coat with a squirrel scarf trailing behind for a tail, executed a dance of quaint steps and low bows. The Dodo jumped or rather walked through three paper hoops, which had to be lowered to admit his chubby person. The King and Queen gave a dialogue, every other line of which was "Off with her head," and the Mad Hatter performed an eccentric dance consisting of marvelous leaps and bounds that took him from one side of the ring to the other with amazing rapidity. When he made his bow the audience shouted with laughter and encored wildly, but with a last nimble skip the panting Hatter made for the Griffon's ladder and, seating himself upon it, refused to respond beyond a nod and a careless wave of his hand. Later he left his perch and proceeded to convulse his audience by sitting on his tall hat and taking a bite from his teacup, the three-cornered bite having been carefully removed beforehand and held temporarily in place with library paste until the proper moment.

As the Mad Hatter, Elfreda was entirely in her element. Her unusually keen sense of humor prompted her to make her impersonation of the immortal Hatter one long to be remembered by those who witnessed the performance given by the famous animals. She was without doubt the feature of the circus and the spectators were quick to note and applaud her slightest movement.

The circus ended with an all-around acrobatic exhibition. The Dodo performed on the trapeze. The Mock Turtle and the Cheshire Cat took turns on a diminutive springboard. The March Hare and the Dormouse energetically jumped over a small barrel. The Queen and the Duchess had a fencing match, the Queen using her sceptre, the Duchess the rag baby she carried, and to which she had sung the "Pepper Song" at intervals during the performance. The King tossed four colored balls into the air, keeping them in motion at once. The Rabbit went on balancing his plate until it slid off his nose, but being tin it struck the ring without breaking. The Griffon lumbered up and down his ladder, while the King and Alice, stepping down to the front of the ring, sang their great duet, "Come, Learn the Way to Wonderland," while, one by one, the animals left off performing their stunts and, surrounding Alice and the King, came out strongly on the chorus:

> "Come, learn the way to Wonderland.
> None of the grown folks understand
> Just where it lies,
> Hid from their eyes.
> 'Tis an enchanted strand
> Where the Hare and the Hatter dance in glee,
> Where curious beasts sit down to tea,
> Where the Mock Turtle sings
> And the Griffon has wings,
> In curious Wonderland."

After the animals had romped out of the ring, and romped in again to take an encore, the audience, who had occupied every reserved seat in the gallery opposite the ring, and packed every available inch of standing room there, came downstairs, while those who had stayed downstairs and peered over one another's shoulders, made a rush for the reserved seat ticket window. Mr. Redfield, the old gentleman who had contributed so liberally to the Semper Fidelis Club, chuckled gleefully over the circus and put in a request that it be given again at the next public entertainment under the auspices of the club.

The second performance was given toward the close of the afternoon, and was even more enthusiastically received. None of the performers left the gymnasium for dinner that night. They preferred to satisfy their hunger at the various booths.

"Oh, there goes Emma," laughed Grace, as late that evening she caught a glimpse of the Egyptian mystery parading majestically down the room ahead of her, then stopping at the Japanese booth to exchange a word with the giggling Emerson twins, who thought the Sphinx the greatest joke imaginable.

A little later as Grace was about to return to the gypsy camp she heard a sudden swish of draperies behind her. Glancing hastily about, she laughed as she saw the Sphinx's unwieldy head towering above her.

"Oh, Great and Wonderful Mystery—" began Grace.

But Emma answered almost crossly: "Don't 'Great and Wonderful Mystery' me. This head is becoming a dead weight, and I'm thirsty and tired, and, besides, something disagreeable just happened."

"What was it?" asked Grace unthinkingly. Then, "I beg your pardon, Emma, I didn't realize the rudeness of my question. Pretend you didn't hear what I said."

"Oh, that is all right," responded Emma laconically. "I don't mind telling you if you will promise on your honor as a junior not to tell a soul."

"I promise," agreed Grace.

"It's about that West person," began Emma disgustedly. "I overheard a conversation between her and her two friends to-night. How did she become so friendly with Alberta Wicks and Mary Hampton? They addressed one another by their first names as though on terms of greatest familiarity."

"I don't know, I am sure," answered Grace slowly. "I seldom see either Miss Wicks or Miss Hampton. When they lived at Stuart Hall I used frequently to pass them on the campus, but since they have been living at Wellington House I rarely, if ever, see either of them. It is just as well, I suppose."

"Thank goodness, this is their last year here," muttered Emma. "We shall have peace during our senior year at least, unless some other disturber appears on the scene."

"Why, Emma Dean!" exclaimed Grace, "what is the matter with you to-night? You aren't a bit like your usual self."

"Then, I'm a successful Sphinx," retorted Emma satirically.

"Of course you are," smiled Grace. "But you can be a successful Sphinx and be yourself, too. But you haven't yet told me anything."

"I'm coming to the information part now," went on Emma. "About an hour ago, while the circus was in full swing, I slipped out of my Sphinx rig and, asking Helen to watch it,—she is made up as the Arab, you know,—I went for a walk around the bazaar. I was sure no one knew that I was the Sphinx, and the Sphinx was I, for I hadn't told a soul except the club girls and Helen. You know I've been purposely taking occasional walks about the gymnasium as Emma Dean. I went over to the Japanese booth for some tea, and while I was drinking it the circus ended and the girls began to pile into the garden for tea. All of a sudden I heard some one say, 'Why didn't you bring your Sphinx costume along, Miss Dean?' It was that horrid little West girl who spoke. Her voice carried, too, for every one in the garden heard her, and they all pounced upon me at once. It made me so angry I rushed out without waiting for my tea, and inside of five minutes the news had circled the gym, and the Sphinx had ceased to be the world's great mystery. I got into the costume again, but the fun was gone. I didn't answer any more questions and I didn't do my dance. I was looking for you to tell you that the Sphinx was about to give up the ghost."

"How could Miss West be so spiteful?" asked Grace vexedly. "Where do you suppose she heard the news, and who told her? You don't suppose—" Grace stopped abruptly. A sudden suspicion had seized her.

"Don't suppose what?" interrogated Emma sharply.

"Nothing," finished Grace shortly.

"Yes, you do suppose something," declared Emma. "I know just what you are thinking. You believe as I do, that Miss West listened—"

"Don't say it, Emma!" exclaimed Grace. "We may both be wrong."

"Then you do believe——"

"I don't know," said Grace bravely. "I admit that suspicion points toward Miss West, but until we know definitely, we must try to be fair-minded. I have seen too much unhappiness result from misplaced suspicion. I know of an instance where a girl was sent to Coventry by her class for almost a year on the merest suspicion."

"Not here?" questioned Emma, her eyes expressing the surprise she felt at this announcement.

"No," returned Grace soberly. There was finality in her "no."

"And the moral is, don't jump at conclusions," smiled Emma. "Come on down to my lair while I remove my Sphinx-like garments and step forth as plain Emma Dean. Don't look so sober, Grace. I've put my suspicions to sleep. I'll give even Miss West the benefit of my doubt. I will even go so far as to forgive her for spoiling my fun to-night. Now smile and say, 'Emma, I always knew you to be the soul of magnanimity.'"

Grace laughed outright at this modest assertion, and obligingly repeated the required words.

"Now that my reputation has been once more established, and because I don't feel half so wrathful as I did ten minutes ago," declared Emma, "let us lay the Sphinx peacefully to rest and do the bazaar arm in arm."

CHAPTER XI

GRACE MEETS WITH A REBUFF

It was several days before the pleasant buzz of excitement created by the bazaar had subsided. With a few exceptions the Overton girls who had turned out, almost in a body, to patronize it, were loud in their praises of the booths, and spent their money with commendable recklessness. Outside the circus it was difficult to say which booth had proved the greatest attraction. But late that evening, after the crowd had gone home and the proceeds of the entertainment were counted, the club discovered to their joy that they were nearly six hundred dollars richer. Arline had laughingly proclaimed the Semper Fidelis Club as a regular get-rich-quick organization with honest motives.

By the time the last bit of frivolous decoration had been removed from the gymnasium, and the big room had recovered its usual business-like air, the bazaar had become a bit of 19—'s history, and Thanksgiving plans were in full swing. There had been two meetings of the club, but to Grace's surprise no mention had been made of Kathleen West's intentional betrayal of Emma Dean's identity. Grace felt certain that the majority of the club had heard the story, and with a thrill of pride she paid tribute to her friends, who, in ignoring the thrust evidently intended for the club itself, had shown themselves as possessors of the true Overton spirit. After Emma's one outburst to Grace against Kathleen she said no more on the subject. Even Elfreda, who usually had something to say about everything when alone with her three friends, was discreetly silent on the subject of the newspaper girl. Long ago she had delivered her ultimatum. To be sure, she went about looking owlishly wise, but she offered no comment concerning Kathleen's unpleasant attitude.

For the time being Grace had put aside all disturbing thoughts and suspicions, and was preparing to make the most of the four days' vacation. Mabel Ashe was to be her guest on Thanksgiving Day, and this in itself was sufficient to banish everything save pleasurable anticipations from her mind. Then, too, there was so much to be done. The Monday evening preceding Thanksgiving Grace hurried through her lessons and, closing her books before she was at all sure that she could make a creditable recitation in any of her subjects, settled herself to the important task of letter-writing.

"There," she announced with satisfaction, after half an hour's steady work, "Father and Mother can't say I forgot them. Let me see, there are Nora and Jessica, Mrs. Gray and Mabel Allison. Eleanor owes me a letter, and, oh, I nearly forgot the Southards, and there is Mrs. Gibson. I shall have to devote two nights to letter-writing," she added ruefully. "I do love to receive letters, but it is so hard to answer them."

"Isn't it, though?" sighed Anne, who was seated at the table opposite Grace, engaged in a similar task. "Now I wish we were going home, don't you, Grace?"

"Yes," returned Grace simply. "But we can't, so there is no use in wishing. However," she continued, her face brightening, "we are going to have Mabel with us, and that means a whole lot. All Overton will be glad to see her—that is, all the juniors and seniors and the faculty and a few others."

"There is only one Mabel Ashe," said Anne softly. "Won't it be splendid to have her with us?"

Grace nodded. Then, after writing busily for a moment, she looked up and said abruptly: "There is just one thing that bothers me, Anne, and that is the way Miss West is behaving. What shall I tell Mabel when she asks me about her? In my letters I haven't made the slightest allusion to anything."

"Tell Mabel the truth," advised Anne calmly. "By that I don't mean that you need mention the Sphinx affair, but if you say to her frankly that we have tried to be friendly with Miss West and that she appears especially to dislike us, she will understand, and nine chances to one she will be able to point out the reason, which so far no one seems to know."

"I suppose I had better tell her," sighed Grace. "I hate to begin a holiday by gossiping, but something will have to be done, or Mabel will find herself in an embarrassing position, for I have a curious presentiment that Miss Kathleen West will pounce upon her the moment she sees her, just to annoy us."

Since the evening of the bazaar, when Kathleen had nodded curtly to Grace at the entrance to the Sphinx's tent, she had neither spoken to nor noticed the four girls who had in the beginning received her so hospitably. No one of them quite understood the newspaper girl's attitude, but as she was often seen in company with Alberta Wicks and Mary Hampton, they were forced to draw their own conclusions. Grace fought against harboring the slightest resemblance to suspicion against the two seniors and their new friend.

"Does Miss West know that Mabel is coming to Overton for Thanksgiving?" asked Anne.

"No," returned Grace, looking rather worried. "I suppose some one ought to tell her."

"I'll tell her, if you like," proposed Anne quietly. "I think she is in her room this evening. I heard her say to one of the girls at dinner that she intended to study hard until late to-night."

"No," decided Grace, "it wouldn't be fair for me to shirk my responsibility. Mabel wrote me about Kathleen West in the first place, and I promised to look out for her. If she doesn't yearn for my society, it isn't my fault. I'm not going to be a coward, at any rate. I'll go at once, while my resolution is at its height. She can't do more than order me from her room, and having been through a similar experience several times in my life I shan't mind it so very much," concluded Grace grimly, closing her fountain pen and laying it beside her half-finished letter. "I'm going now, Anne. I hope she won't be too difficult."

Grace walked resolutely down the hall to the door at the end. It was slightly ajar. Rapping gently, she stood waiting, bravely stifling the strong inclination to turn and walk away without delivering her message. She heard a quick step; then she and Kathleen West confronted each other. Without hesitating, Grace said frankly: "Miss

West, Miss Ashe is to be my guest on Thanksgiving Day. Of late you have avoided me, and my friends as well. But Mabel is our mutual friend. So I think, at least while she is here, we ought to put all personal differences aside and unite in making the day pleasant for her."

"Nothing like being disinterested, is there?" broke in the other girl sneeringly, her sharp face looking sharper than ever. "I can quite understand your anxiety regarding not letting Miss Ashe know how shabbily you have treated me. Your promises to her didn't hold water, did they? And now you are afraid she will find you out, aren't you? Don't worry, I shan't tell her. She'll learn the truth about you and your three friends soon enough."

"You know very well I had no such motive," cried Grace, surprised to indignation. "Besides, I know of no instance in which either my friends or I have failed in courtesy to you."

"How innocent you are!" mimicked Kathleen insolently. "You must think me very blind. Remember, I haven't worked for four years on a newspaper without having learned a few things."

Grace felt her color rising. The retort that rose to her lips found its way into speech. "No doubt your newspaper work has taught you a great deal, Miss West," she said evenly, "but I have not been in college for over two years without having learned a few things, also, of which, if I am not mistaken, you have never acquired even the first rudiments. I am sorry to have troubled you. Good night."

With a proud little inclination of the head, Grace turned and walked down the hall to her own room, leaving the self-centered Kathleen with an angry color in her thin face and the unpleasant knowledge that though she might be in college, she was not of it.

CHAPTER XII

THANKSGIVING AT OVERTON

In spite of the awkwardness of the situation precipitated by the belligerent newspaper girl, Thanksgiving Day passed off with remarkable smoothness. Greatly to Grace's surprise, in the morning after Mabel's arrival at Wayne Hall Kathleen West had appeared in the living-room where Mabel was holding triumphant court, greeted her with apparent cordiality, and after remaining in the room for a short time had pleaded an engagement for the day, and said good-bye.

"Too bad she couldn't stay with us and go to the game, isn't it?" Mabel had declared regretfully. "I suppose she is obliged to divide her time. Miss West is so clever. She must be very popular?" she added inquiringly.

At that moment Elfreda purposely began an account of the latest practice game in which her team had played, and Mabel, who was an ardent basketball fan, failed to notice that her questioning comment had been neither answered nor echoed. To the relief of the four friends the subject of Kathleen West was not renewed during Mabel's stay, and when, that night, she went to the station surrounded by a large and faithful bodyguard, all adverse criticism against the girl for whom she had spoken was locked within the breasts of the four who knew.

On the Friday after Thanksgiving the first real game between the freshmen and the sophomore teams took place in the gymnasium. The freshmen won the game, much to Elfreda's disgust, as she had pinned her faith on the sophomores. The triumphant team marched around the gymnasium, lustily singing a ridiculously funny basketball song which it afterward developed had been composed by none other than Kathleen West.

"Too bad she isn't up to her song," had been Elfreda's dry comment, with which the other three girls privately agreed.

The Morton House girls issued tickets for a play, which had to be postponed because the leading man (Gertrude Wells) spent Thanksgiving in the country and missed the afternoon train to Overton. Nothing daunted, Arline descended upon Grace, Miriam and Anne, pressed them into service and sent them scurrying about to the houses and boarding places of the girls they knew to be at home, with eleventh-hour invitations to a fancy dress party to be held at Morton Hall in lieu of the play, which had to be postponed until the following week. Arline had stipulated that the costumes must be strictly original. Wonderland costumes were to be tabooed. "If we present the circus again later on we don't want to run the risk of giving any one the slightest chance to grow tired of seeing the animals," had been her wise edict.

That night a mixed company of gay and gallant folks danced to the music of the living-room piano at Morton House. Those receiving invitations had immediately planned their costumes and by eight o'clock that evening, resplendent in their own and borrowed finery, were on their way to the ball. At ten o'clock there had been a brief intermission, when cakes and ices were served. This had been an unlooked-for courtesy on the part of Arline, who had plunged recklessly into her month's allowance for the purchase of the little spread. The ball had lasted until half-past eleven o'clock, and the participants, after singing to Arline and rendering her a noisy vote of thanks, had gone home tired and happy.

Saturday had been devoted to the "odds and ends" of vacation. The majority of the girls, having stayed in Overton, paid long-deferred calls, gave luncheons or dinners at Vinton's or Martell's, or, the day being unusually clear, went for long walks. Guest House was the destination of a party of girls of whom Grace made one, and which also included Miriam, Elfreda, Laura Atkins, Violet Darby and half a dozen other young women who had elected the five-mile walk, supper, and a return by moonlight. Arline, Anne and Ruth had at the last moment decided to attend an illustrated lecture on Paris, to be held in the Overton Theatre that afternoon, with the gleeful prospect of cooking their supper at Ruth's that evening, an occasion invariably attended with at least one laughable mishap, as neither

Arline's nor Anne's knowledge of cooking extended beyond the art of boiling water.

On the way back from Guest House the pedestrians had stopped at Vinton's for a rest and ices. As they trooped in the door, they passed Kathleen West, accompanied by Alberta Wicks, Mary Hampton, and a freshman whom Grace had frequently noticed in company with the newspaper girl. Several of the girls with her bowed to the passing trio, but Grace fancied there was a lack of cordiality in their salutations. She also imagined she noticed a fleeting gleam of malice in Alberta Wicks's face as the senior passed their table. Inwardly censuring herself for allowing any such impression to creep into her mind, Grace dismissed it with an impatient little shake of the head.

The walking party indulged in a second round of ices before leaving Vinton's. Everyone seemed to be in a particularly happy mood, and long afterward Grace looked back on this night as one of the particular occasions of her junior year, when everyone and everything seemed to be in absolute harmony.

All the way home this exalted, elated mood remained with her. She smiled to herself as she leisurely prepared for bed at the recollection of her happy evening. Elfreda's sharp, familiar knock on the door caused her to start slightly, then she called, "Come in!"

"Hasn't Anne come home yet?" asked Elfreda, glancing about her, then, shuffling across the room in her satin mules, she curled herself comfortably on the end of Grace's couch, and, surveying Grace with friendly, half-quizzical eyes, said shrewdly, "Well, what's the latest on the bulletin board?"

"I don't know," smiled Grace. "I didn't look at the one in the hall and as for the one over at the college, I haven't paid any attention to it for the last two days. My letters usually come to Wayne Hall."

Elfreda sniffed disdainfully. "I don't mean either of those bulletin boards, and you know it, too, Grace Harlowe. I could see danger signals flying to-night, even if you couldn't. I don't see how you could have missed them." She eyed Grace searchingly, then said, with conviction, "I don't believe you did miss them. They were too plain to be missed."

Grace hesitated, then said frankly: "To tell you the truth, Elfreda, I did fancy for a moment that Miss Wicks favored me with a very peculiar look. Then I decided it to be a case of imagination on my part. Those girls haven't troubled us this year. I don't know — —" she began slowly.

Elfreda interrupted her with an emphatic: "That is just what I've been telling you. That's what I mean by danger signals. Those two girls will never forgive you for making them ridiculous the night they locked me in the haunted house. Last year they had to content themselves with simply being disagreeable, because they could find no particularly weak spot in our sophomore armor. They accomplished very little with Laura Atkins and Mildred Taylor. This year it's different." Elfreda paused to give full effect to her words. Then she ended slowly and impressively: "Don't think I'm trying to court calamity, but I am certain that perky little newspaper woman, as she styles herself, is going to prove a thorn in your side. You had better write to Mabel and explain matters, then leave Miss Kathleen West alone. She hasn't spoken to you since the day of the bazaar, so I can't see that your junior counsel is of any particular use to her."

"Still, it seems a shame to give up; besides, it is the first thing Mabel ever asked me to do," demurred Grace.

"I know, I've thought of that," continued Elfreda a little impatiently. "But I don't think you are justified in wasting your whole year's fun worrying about some one who isn't worth it. If Mabel knew, she would be the first one to indorse what I have just said."

"I'm not wasting my year, Elfreda mine," contradicted Grace good-naturedly. "Just think what a nice time we had to-night! And I'm getting along splendidly with all my subjects. I belong to the Semper Fidelis Club, and am having the jolliest kind of times with you girls. That doesn't sound much like wasting my year, does it?"

"I didn't say you had wasted it," retorted Elfreda gruffly. "I said, or rather intended to say, that you would be likely to waste it. You are the sort of girl who ought to have the best Overton can offer, because—well—because you deserve it. You think too much about other people, and not enough about yourself," she concluded shortly.

"What a selfish Elfreda," laughed Grace, walking across the room and sitting down beside the stout girl, whose round face looked unusually severe. "One might think Elfreda Briggs never did an unselfish act in all her twenty-two years. Now I am going to give you a piece of your own advice. Stop worrying—about me. Whatever my just desserts are, they'll overtake me fast enough. Hurrah! Here is our little Anne. Did you have a nice time, dear, and what did you cook for supper?"

"I always have a nice time at Ruth's," smiled Anne, "but, if you had seen the three cooks all trying to spoil the broth and succeeding beyond their wildest expectations, you would have been greatly edified."

"I can imagine Arline Thayer gravely bending over that little gas stove of Ruth's," said Grace.

"She had all sorts of splendid ideas about what we might make, but no one had the slightest idea as to how to make anything she proposed."

"I am afraid none of us would ever set the world on fire as cooks," observed Elfreda with sarcasm.

"Where's Miriam?" asked Anne, slipping out of her coat and unpinning her hat.

"Writing to her mother," returned Elfreda. "Now tell us what you cooked."

Frequent bursts of laughter arose as Anne described Arline's valiant attempt at making a Spanish omelet from a recipe in a cook-book she had purchased that very day for twenty-five cents at the little book store just below the campus. "It was called the 'Model Housewife,' but the omelet was really a dreadful affair," continued Anne. "Then I let the potatoes boil dry and they scorched on the bottom, and no one knew how to make a cream dressing for the peas.

"Ruth made a Waldorf salad. We had a bottle of dressing, thank goodness. And Arline made coffee, which she really does know how to make. We had olives and pickles and cakes, and two dozen of those cunning little rolls from that German bakery down the street. So we really managed to get enough to eat after all. There wasn't much left except the omelet, and no one wanted that."

"I don't suppose it would be of the least use to propose tea," said Grace innocently.

"Well, of course, if you insist," declared Elfreda politely.

At this juncture Miriam appeared in the door. "I thought I'd drop in for a minute. You were making so much noise I suspected that a tea party was in progress," she said significantly.

"We were just talking about making tea," declared Anne. "In fact, I was on the point of remarking that tea was really the one thing needed to complete our happiness."

A little gust of laughter greeted this pointed remark. It echoed down the hall, and was carried through the half-opened door of the room at the end, where a girl sat busily engaged in writing a theme. She lay down her pen, listened for a moment, then went on writing, a sarcastic little smile playing about her lips. But in her eyes flashed two danger signals.

CHAPTER XIII

ARLINE MAKES THE BEST OF A BAD MATTER

"What shall we do for our eight girls this year?" asked Grace reflectively of Arline Thayer. It was barely two weeks until Christmas and the two girls had decided to spend their half holiday in doing the Overton stores.

"I know the stock better than the saleswomen themselves do," chuckled Arline, "but it is great fun to go on exploring expeditions and watch other people buy the things. Of course, I always buy something, too, unless I am deep in that state of temporary poverty that lies in wait for me at the end of every month."

"Of course you do," agreed Grace, with an answering chuckle. "Even though it is a hat and you feel obliged to dispose of it before going home, so that the Morton House girls won't laugh at you."

"Who told you about it?" asked Arline in a half-vexed tone.

"You told me, don't you remember?" asked Grace.

"Oh, yes, of course. Wasn't I a goose?"

"Thank you," bowed Grace mockingly.

"Oh, I don't mean because I told you," apologized Arline hastily. "I mean, wasn't I a goose to buy it? It was in this very store. It looked so pretty. I was determined to have it. Outside the store it looked quite different. It was a perfectly honest dollar-and-a-half hat. But in the store under the electric lights it was really a pretentious affair. Ruth was with me at the time, and, wise little pilot that she is, tried to steer me past it. But I was determined to have it. After I left Ruth, I opened the box and looked at it in broad daylight, and then I happened to meet my washerwoman's daughter, and I gave it to her. It was so fortunate I met her, wasn't it?" finished Arline plaintively.

"For the washerwoman's daughter, yes," returned Grace.

"It served me right for buying it. I spend too much money foolishly," said Arline self-accusingly. "I'm going to stop being so reckless. Suppose my father were to lose all his money and I couldn't even come back to college next year? I would, though. I'd go and live with Ruth and borrow enough money of the Semper Fidelis Club to see me through my senior year. Then, I suppose, I'd have to teach or something afterward. I think it would be 'or something.' I don't believe teaching is my vocation."

Grace listened in smiling silence to Arline's remarks. A vision of the little blue-eyed golden-haired girl who always did exactly as she pleased in the prim guise of a teacher was infinitely diverting.

"You haven't answered my question about our girls yet," reminded Grace, as they walked down the center aisle of the larger of the two Overton stores, stopping frequently at the various counters to examine the display of holiday wares.

"Haven't you any suggestions?" counter-questioned Arline. "I have been depending on you for inspiration."

"Nothing new or original," answered Grace doubtfully. "Last year's stunt was beautifully carried out, but we can't repeat it this year without running the risk of some one finding out just who our eight girls are and all about them. Then, too, what we did last year was on the spur of the moment. If we tried to do the same thing this year it might fall flat, on account of being too carefully planned. Besides, these girls have the privilege of borrowing from the Semper Fidelis fund now, and I imagine most of them have done so. Of course, only the treasurer knows that."

"It looks to me as though there were more real need of a little Christmas cheer," declared Arline thoughtfully. "Couldn't we arrange some kind of entertainment to take place before we all go?"

"But that wouldn't seem much like Christmas unless it happened on Christmas Day," objected Grace. "We'll all be at home then."

"Why not have a talk with Miss Barlow?" proposed Arline eagerly. "You are the one to do it. You know her better than I do. Suppose we call upon her within the next few days. Then you can find out what she and her friends intend to do. If she says they are all going to stay here, then ask her if she wouldn't like to—" Arline paused and looked rather helplessly at Grace. "That's as far as I can go," she confessed. "I haven't the least idea of what I should ask her."

"I am equally destitute of ideas," agreed Grace. "Perhaps the inspiration is yet to come."

"It will have to come soon then, or we won't have the time to carry it out," commented Arline dryly. "Keep it in mind, and if you think of anything let me know instantly, won't you?"

Grace gave the desired promise and thought no more of it until she and Arline almost came into violent collision just outside the library the following Monday evening.

"Grace Harlowe!" exclaimed the little girl. "I was coming to Wayne Hall to see you the instant I finished here. It has come, Grace! The great inspiration! But it is a dreadful disappointment to me." Several big tears chased each other down Arline's rosy cheeks. Her lip quivered, and with a little, choking sob she sat down on the lowest step of the library and began to cry softly.

"Arline, dear child, whatever is the matter?" cried Grace in quick alarm. A moment later she had slipped to the step beside Arline, passing one arm about her friend's shoulder. She could scarcely believe this weeping, disconsolate little creature to be the smiling, self-assured Arline Thayer, who was forever receiving flowers from admiring freshmen crushes.

"Father's going to—Europe—on—important business," quavered Arline brokenly. "He—he sails to-morrow morning and he can't possibly return before the middle of January." She raised her sad little face to Grace's sympathetic one, then, straightening up, she went on bravely, "We had so many lovely Christmas plans."

"Come home with me, Arline," begged Grace. "I'd love to have you."

Arline shook her blonde head, at the same time slipping her hand into Grace's. "I thought of that, too," she returned softly. "I was going to ask you if I might go home with you for Christmas. Then Ruth and I had a talk. I had asked her to go home with me, and she had refused because she is so afraid of outwearing her welcome. Then came Father's letter. Ruth was a dear about that. She said at once that if I wished to go home and felt that I needed her she would go, but I couldn't bear to think of spending Christmas in that big, lonely house. It is Father that makes it seem so wonderful to go home." Arline's lip quivered piteously. "He and I could be happy if we were the poorest of the poor. You must visit me some time, Grace. Perhaps we could have an Easter house party. Wouldn't that be splendid?" Arline's woe-be-gone face brightened. Grace patted her hand.

"Get up, Arline, before some one sees you," she advised. "Whoever heard of proud little Daffydowndilly Thayer crying like an ordinary mortal?" Grace went on soothing Arline in this half-serious fashion, which presently had its effect.

"You are so comforting, Grace," sighed Arline, as she rose from the steps, an expression of gratitude in her pretty blue eyes. "Can't you walk over to the house with me? I want you to hear my plan and tell me what you think of it."

"I could put off my library business until to-morrow," reflected Grace, smiling a little. "It will be a case of doing as I please instead of doing as I ought. Still, as a loyal member of Semper Fidelis it is my duty to comfort my sorrowing comrades. Don't you think so?"

Arline laughed an almost happy response to Grace's question.

"But I mustn't stay long," warned Grace a little later, as, seated opposite Arline in the latter's room, she awaited the unfolding of Arline's "inspiration."

"I'm going to stay here for Christmas," announced Arline with the finality of one who knows her own mind. "Ruth is coming up to live with me for the whole vacation, too. That isn't the inspiration, though. That is only the first part of it. The second part is that Ruth and I are going to see to the eight girls, and all the others who aren't going away from Overton. What do you think of that?"

"I think it is dear in you, Arline," responded Grace very earnestly. "I only wish I might stay to help you. However, Father and Mother have first claim on my vacation. But let me help you plan and get things ready before I go. I'll be here until a week from next Thursday, you know."

"Oh, I shall need you," Arline assured Grace. "I thought we might have Christmas dinner at Vinton's and Martell's, too. I've thought it all out. Both restaurants depend largely on the Overton girls' patronage. Naturally, they are very dull at Christmas time. My idea was to interview both proprietors and see if for once they wouldn't combine and furnish the same menu at the same price per plate, the price to be not more than fifty cents. It must be just an old-fashioned turkey dinner with plenty of dressing and vegetables. We must have plum pudding, too, and all the things that go with a real Christmas dinner."

"But neither Vinton's nor Martell's would serve that sort of Christmas dinner for fifty cents," said Grace slowly. "I don't wish to discourage you, but—"

"I know that, too," broke in Arline eagerly, "but no one else need know. I'm going to take my check that Father always gives me for theatres and things when I'm at home, and spend it to make up the difference. It will more than cover the extra expense of the dinner. I'd like to give the dinner to the girls, but of course that is out of the question. They wouldn't like it. However, if they are allowed to pay fifty cents for it they will feel independent, and, nine chances out of ten, won't trouble themselves about the actual cost of the dinner, as have some persons I might mention," ended Arline meaningly.

Both girls laughed. Then Grace said admiringly: "It is a splendidly unselfish idea, and you and Ruth are the very ones to carry it out. Shall you have a play or anything afterward?"

"Yes, if we can find a good one. I thought we might have a New Year's masquerade party here. It will be an innovation for these girls. I am not very sure of anything yet, except that I am not going to New York and that I must do something to amuse myself while the rest of my friends are reposing in the bosoms of their families. After all, mine is really a selfish motive," said the little girl whimsically.

"Hush!" exclaimed Grace, laying her hand lightly against Arline's lips. "I shall not allow you to say slighting things of yourself. I have just one remark to make. Be very diplomatic, Arline. If any of these girls who can't afford to go home for the holidays were even to imagine themselves objects of charity, your dinner plan would be a failure. Don't tell a soul about it except Ruth."

"I know," nodded Arline wisely. "I had thought of that, too. Never fear, I won't breathe it to another soul."

"My half hour is more than up," exclaimed Grace ruefully, glancing toward the little French clock on Arline's chiffonier. "I must hurry away this instant. I'll see you again in a day or two. I am so sorry for your disappointment. You're the bravest little Daffydowndilly. If my prospects of going home were suddenly swept away, I'm afraid I'd be too busy with my own woes to think about making other people happy."

"You would do just what I am planning to do, Grace Harlowe," declared Arline emphatically. "After all, perhaps it is just as well I can't always have my own way. I might become a monument of selfishness."

"There doesn't seem to be much danger of it," laughed Grace, as she put on her hat and slipped into her long coat. "There is a strong possibility, however, that 'not prepared' will be my watchword to-morrow. I think I shall write a theme on the decline of the art of study and use personal illustrations. It seems such a shame that mid-years had to come skulking along on the very heels of Christmas, doesn't it?"

Arline nodded. "I haven't looked at my French for to-morrow, either," she confessed, "and I've been saying 'not prepared' for the last two recitations. Ruth and I have planned a systematic study campaign during vacation, so you see the ill wind will blow some little good," she concluded wistfully.

Grace smiled very tenderly at the little, golden-haired girl who was bearing her cross bravely, almost gayly. "Good-night, little Daffydowndilly," she said impulsively, bending to kiss Arline's rosy cheek. "I think you can teach all of us a lesson in real unselfishness."

CHAPTER XIV

PLANNING THE CHRISTMAS DINNER

The ensuing days before Christmas were filled to the brim with business for Grace and Arline, who had been making secret tours of investigation about Overton with regard to the girls who were not going to their homes or to friends for the vacation. The managers at Martell's and Vinton's had been interviewed, and both proprietors had agreed to furnish practically the same dinner at the same price, which was considerably more than fifty cents, and was to be paid privately from Arline's own pocket money.

"I feel like a conspirator," confided Arline to Grace as the two girls sat at the library table in the living room at Wayne Hall late one afternoon going over a long list of names and addresses which they had obtained by dint of much walking and inquiring.

"But it is such a delightful conspiracy," reminded Grace. "One doesn't often conspire to make other people happy. I hope the girls will fall in readily with your plan."

"I shall have to be as wise as a serpent," smiled Arline, "and as diplomatic as—as—Miriam Nesbit. She is the most diplomatic person I ever knew."

"Isn't she, though?" agreed Grace smilingly. "Yes, my dear Daffydowndilly, you have a delicate task before you. Playing Lady Bountiful to the girls who are left behind without them suspecting you won't be easy. There are certain girls who would languish in their rooms all day, rather than accept a mouthful of food that savored of charity. I don't believe our eight girls ever suspected us of playing Santa Claus to them last year."

"Oh, I am certain they never knew," returned Arline quickly. "Of course, there was a remote chance that they and the various girls, who contributed might compare notes. But those who gave presents and money were in honor bound not to ask questions or even discuss the matter among themselves. I know the Morton House girls never said a word, too."

"Neither did the Wayne Hallites," rejoined Grace. "Even Miriam, Anne and Elfreda asked no questions."

"Doesn't it seem wonderful to think that girls can be so splendidly impersonal and honorable?" commented Arline admiringly. "College is the very place to cultivate that attitude. Living up to college traditions means being honorable in the highest sense of the word. There are plenty of girls who come here without realizing what being an Overton girl means, until they find themselves face to face with the fact that their standards are not high enough. That is why one hears so much about finding one's self. College is like a great mirror. When one first enters it, one takes a quick glance at one's self and is pleased with the effect. Later, when one stops for a more comprehensive survey, one discovers all sorts of imperfections, and it takes four years of constant striving with one's self as well as one's studies to make a satisfactory reflection."

"What a quaint idea!" exclaimed Grace. "We might evolve a play from that and call it 'The Magic Mirror.' That would be a stunt for a show. Miriam Nesbit could do a college girl. She looks the part. But here, I am miles off my subject. Suppose we go back to our girls. How are you going to propose the dinner plan, Arline?"

"I'm going to wait until every last girl that is going home has departed, bag and baggage; then I shall post a bulletin on the big board, asking all the stay-heres to meet me in the gymnasium," planned Arline. "I shall say that as I am going to stay over and didn't fancy eating my Christmas dinner alone I thought perhaps the girls who had no particular plans for the day would like to join me at either Martell's or Vinton's. Then I'll explain about the price of the dinner, etc., all in a perfectly offhand manner, and let them do the rest. There are anywhere from one to two hundred girls who live at the various rooming and boarding houses who will be glad to come. Many of them have never been inside either Vinton's or Martell's. You would hardly believe it, but it's true."

"I do believe it," said Grace soberly. "It seems a shame, too, when I think of the amount of time and money we spend there."

"Well, I haven't grown philanthropic enough to give up going to either one," declared Arline. "They are my havens of refuge when Morton House cooking deteriorates, as it frequently does. Ask me for my cloak or even my best new pumps, but don't tear me away from my favorite haunts."

"I won't," promised Grace. "I am afraid I feel the same. No chance for reformation along that line. Shall we send the eight girls gifts or a present of money this year, or both?"

"I suspect they have all borrowed from the Semper Fidelis fund this year," was Arline's quick answer. "Suppose we send presents, and ask our club girls alone to contribute toward them. If every one we asked gave two dollars apiece, that would mean twenty-four dollars. We could invest it in gloves, neckwear and pretty things that most poor girls are obliged to do without. We gave money last year because those girls had no one to help them. This year Semper Fidelis stands behind them. Besides, some one might find it out this time. I said I was certain they never knew, but I always had a curious idea that Miss Barlow suspected you, Grace. Whenever I meet her she always speaks of you with positive reverence."

A flush rose to Grace's face. "How ridiculous," she murmured. "You are the real heroine of that adventure. Have you decided on your programme for the week yet?"

"Only the costume party and a basketball game, if we can scare up two teams, and a winter picnic at Hunter's Rock, if it isn't too cold. A play, if we can gather up enough actors, and a dance in the gymnasium. I'm going to give an afternoon tea, and that's all, I think. They will have to amuse themselves the rest of the time," finished Arline with a sigh. "There are so many ifs attached to my plans."

"I predict a busy two weeks for you," said Grace, "but then—"

From the room adjoining, which opened into the living room and was used as a parlor, came the sound of a slight cough. Grace was on her feet in an instant. With a bound she sprang toward the curtained archway and, pushing it aside, peered sharply into the room. It was empty.

"Did you hear some one cough, Arline?" she asked anxiously.

"Yes," replied Arline, who had joined her. "The sound came from in here, didn't it?"

"So I imagined," declared Grace in a puzzled tone. "Perhaps it came from the hall. No one could have escaped from here before I reached the door without my hearing them. It startled me, because we had been talking so confidentially. I glanced in as we passed the door when we went into the living room and there wasn't a soul in sight. Whoever coughed a few moments ago must have slipped into the room and slipped out again."

"Then, whoever it is has heard the very things we didn't wish known!" exclaimed Arline in consternation. "Now I can't carry out any of my plans. How perfectly dreadful!"

"Perhaps it was Mrs. Elwood," said Grace hopefully.

"Mrs. Elwood is far too stout to walk so lightly and vanish so rapidly," discouraged Arline. "I—it—must have been some one who was trying to hear."

"If that is the case, the person is in this house and must be found and sworn to secrecy," said Grace sternly. "I am afraid we were talking too loudly. However, the person may have only come as far as the door, then passed on upstairs. Suppose we go up and ask all the girls. We shall feel better satisfied, and they won't object to being interviewed."

But all efforts to locate the accidental or intentional listener failed. Many of the girls had not yet come in from their classes, and those whom Grace found in their rooms had evidently been there for some time. Kathleen West was among those still out. Miss Ainslee informed her visitors of this fact with an unmistakable sigh of relief that Grace interpreted with a slight smile. As she went slowly down the stairs to the living room, followed by Arline, whose baby face wore an expression of deepest gloom, the door bell rang and the maid admitted the newspaper girl. She swept past the two juniors who stood at the foot of the stairs without the slightest sign of recognition, and neither girl saw the look of triumph that animated her face the instant she had turned her back upon them and hurried up the stairs.

"What shall we do?" asked Arline as once more they seated themselves at the library table opposite each other.

"We can't do anything until we find the girl who listened, and the question is how are we to find her?" Grace made a little gesture of despair.

Arline shrugged her dainty shoulders. "I don't know. Perhaps she will never repeat what she has heard. Curiosity alone may have prompted her to listen. We may be agreeably disappointed."

Grace shook her head. "I wish I could believe that," she said. "I don't wish to croak, but I have a curious conviction that the person who listened had a motive deeper than mere curiosity."

CHAPTER XV

A TISSUE PAPER TEA

"What in the name of all mysterious is going on between you and Alice-In-Wonderland Daffydowndilly Thayer?" demanded Elfreda Briggs as she lovingly wrapped a large pasteboard box in white tissue paper and tied it with a huge bow of scarlet satin ribbon. "This is Miriam's present," she drawled calmly. "You will observe that she has obligingly turned her back while I am engaged in wrestling with wrapping it. I never could tie a bow. I have had this box in the closet for a week, and it has fallen out every time we opened the door, but Miriam, beloved angel, hasn't shown the slightest curiosity. You may look, my dear, the big box is all put away," she declared, as though addressing a very small child.

"What a ridiculous person you are, J. Elfreda Briggs," laughed Miriam. "One might think me at the kindergarten age, instead of your guardian and keeper."

"Tell me what it is, Elfreda," teased Grace.

"On one condition," answered Elfreda, reaching for a small square box and beginning to wrap it in holly paper. "Tell me what you and Arline are planning!"

"It's a secret," returned Grace. "I'd love to tell you, but I am pledged until the day we go home. When we are all in the train and it has started on the home stretch then you shall know."

"There is no time like the present," invited Elfreda.

"No," laughed Grace, shaking her head. "Not now. I have given my promise to Arline."

"She won't tell even me," smiled Anne Pierson, who, with Grace, had carried her Christmas gifts to Miriam's and Elfreda's room, in answer to Elfreda's invitation to a tissue paper tea. "Bring all your stuff," Elfreda directed. "There will be plenty of paper and ribbon and twine and tea and cakes if I have time to go for them." Cheered with the prospect of tea and cakes, which were a certainty in spite of Elfreda's provisional promise, the two guests had come, their arms full of bundles.

"Well, if she won't tell *you*, the rest of us might as well save our breath," declared Elfreda. "Never mind, we have only two more days to wait. Oh, aren't you glad you're going home? I have been homesick for the last three days. I'm glad we are going to stay in Fairview and have an old-fashioned Christmas. I am going to drive to the woods and cut down my own Christmas tree, too."

"That reminds me, Miriam, we must make up a party and go to Upton Wood to see old Jean. We didn't see him last summer on account of his being away up in northwestern Canada. He went as a guide. Don't you remember? In Mother's last letter she wrote that he had been seen in Oakdale. That means that he has come back to his cabin in Upton Wood."

"Hurrah!" exclaimed Miriam, waving a long, narrow package over her head. "That means a winter picnic, and supper at old Jean's cabin."

"Who is old Jean?" asked Elfreda curiously.

"Come down to Oakdale between Christmas and New Year and go with us on the picnic," teased Miriam. "You can see old Jean for yourself."

"Can't do it," responded Elfreda. "I am strictly Pa's and Ma's girl this time. I've promised."

"Then I suppose I shall have to enlighten you," smiled Grace. "Jean is an old Frenchman, a hunter who drifted down to Oakdale from somewhere in Canada. He has a log cabin in Upton Wood, a forest just east of Oakdale. To him I owe the beautiful set of fox furs, you have so often admired. He had the skins dressed for me, and Mother sent them to a furrier's in New York and had them made into a muff and scarf for me. I have known him since I was a little girl."

"Lucky you," commented Elfreda. "There, I've finished my packages. I'm going out to buy cakes. You have worked nobly. This

Saturday afternoon, at least, has been well spent, thanks to my tissue paper tea. Now we'll have real tea." Piling her smaller packages into a neat heap, she made a dive for her long brown coat and fur cap. "Don't dare to touch one of those packages. You might guess what is in them. Good-bye. I'll be back before you know it."

As the door closed after her with a resounding bang, Miriam remarked affectionately: "Elfreda is in her element. She loves to play hostess and give tea parties."

"She is becoming one of the important girls in college, isn't she?" observed Anne. "I was so glad to see her rushed by the Phi Beta Gammas."

"She was more moved than she would admit over being asked to join them," returned Miriam. "She used to make ridiculous remarks about them and call them the P. B. Gammas, but in her heart she looked upon them with positive awe. Wasn't it nice to think we were all asked?"

"I should say so," agreed Grace. "It would have been dreadful if one of us had been left out." She patted her sorority pin with intense satisfaction. "In spite of belonging to the most important sorority in college, there never will be another sorority like the Phi Sigma Tau, will there, girls?"

"No," said Miriam, smiling with a reminiscent tenderness at sound of the familiar name.

"Dear old P. S. T.," murmured Anne. "How I wish we might call a meeting now and have every member present."

"There is bound to be one vacant place when we gather home next week," said Grace a trifle sadly.

"The Lady Eleanor," sighed Miriam. "I hope we'll see her some time next year."

The arrival of Elfreda, her arms filled with bundles, cut short Miriam's reflections. One by one Elfreda calmly laid down her packages and began preparations for her tissue paper tea. The stout girl's mood seemed to have changed, however. She answered her companions' gay sallies rather abstractedly, with the air of one whose thoughts were anywhere but on her guests. Several times Grace glanced up to find Elfreda's eyes fixed reflectively upon her.

When, at five o'clock, she announced her intention of going for a walk before dinner, Elfreda gave her another peculiar look and announced her intention of accompanying her. Anne and Miriam, who had elected to occupy the time before dinner in writing to the Southards, declined Grace's invitation, and as the two girls walked briskly down the street, Elfreda breathed a deep sigh of relief. "With all due respect to Miriam and Anne, I am glad they didn't join us," she said coolly.

"What is on your mind now?" asked Grace shrewdly.

"So you realize at last that there is something on my mind, do you!" retorted Elfreda grimly. "I began to think you never could. I made all kinds of signals to you with my eyes."

"I thought they were signals, but wasn't sure," said Grace quickly.

"Well, you can be sure now. I don't want you to think me a Paul Pry, but I know all about that Christmas business last year."

"What 'Christmas business'?" asked Grace sharply.

"You know very well what I mean, the eight girls and all that."

"Why—who——" began Grace in displeased astonishment.

"No, I didn't try to find out," interrupted Elfreda. "You know me better than that. No one told me, either. I just put two and two together. I could see last year that——"

"Is there anything you can't see?" exclaimed Grace.

"Not much," responded Elfreda modestly. "I knew, of course, you would do something for those girls this year."

"You could see that, I suppose," said Grace satirically.

"Exactly," nodded Elfreda with an irresistible grin. Their eyes meeting, both girls laughed. Elfreda's face sobered first. "My news isn't pleasant, Grace. Read this." Slipping her hand into her coat pocket she drew forth a half sheet of paper partly covered with writing. Grace received it wonderingly:

"Two Overton College Girls Play Lady Bountiful to Their Needy Classmates," she read. The words were arranged to form headlines, and below was written: "The latest whim of two wealthy students of Overton College has taken the form of Sweet Charity, and impecunious students of Overton whose finances will not permit of their making long railway journeys home for Christmas are to be the object of these young women's solicitude. Their less fortunate classmates will be their guests at a dinner on Christmas which by special arrangement will be served at— —" The writing ended with the bottom of the sheet.

"What do you think of that?" demanded Elfreda laconically.

A tide of crimson rose to Grace's face. "I think it is contemptible," she cried. "When and where did you find it, Elfreda?"

"Just outside the door of the room at the end of the hall," replied Elfreda. "I picked it up as I was coming back from the delicatessen shop."

Grace's eyes flashed. "I suspected as much," she said shortly. "What does this look like to you, Elfreda?"

"Newspaper copy," replied Elfreda promptly. "It isn't the first, either. I happen to know she writes college stuff and sends it to her paper every week. I knew that long ago. I subscribed to the Sunday edition of her paper on purpose. I know her articles, too. She signs them 'Elizabeth Vassar.' I have been quietly censoring them all along, ready to object if she once overstepped the line. So far she hasn't. I didn't know this was her copy until I had read it. Then it dawned upon me what the whole thing meant. This is the beginning of an article designed purely for spite. It is a direct stab at you and Arline. I suppose certain other people have influenced her against you, Grace. These very people will see to the circulation of the paper here at Overton, too, when the article appears, or I'm no prophet."

"I suppose so," assented Grace almost wearily. "I am sure I can't think of any reason other than spite for this." She took a few steps in silence, her eyes bent on the sheet of paper.

"You had better hurry and do something about this," advised Elfreda, lightly touching the paper with her forefinger, "or it will be too late."

Grace glanced up with a slight start.

"Once she finds the first of her copy missing it won't take her long to rewrite it," reminded Elfreda. "She may have mailed it by this time, although I hardly think so. I am afraid you will have trouble with her. She looks like one of the do-as-I-please-in-spite-of-you kind. What's the matter, Grace? What makes you look so funny?"

"I know where I saw it!" exclaimed Grace enigmatically, apparently deaf to Elfreda's questions. "It was in the note. She wrote it. Strange I never thought of that."

"Grace Harlowe," demanded Elfreda with asperity, "have you suddenly taken leave of your senses?"

"No," returned Grace, her gray eyes gleaming wrathfully, her lips set in a determined line as she faced about. "I've just found them. Yes, Elfreda, I shall certainly call on Miss West, and at once."

CHAPTER XVI

A DOUBTFUL VICTORY

During the walk to Wayne Hall, Elfreda could scarcely keep pace with Grace's flying feet. She made no complaint, however, but kept sturdily at her companion's side, holding her breath and closing her lips tightly to keep from panting. Grace ran into her own room for a moment, then back to Elfreda, who stood waiting in the upstairs hall.

"Shall I leave you here?" she asked in a low tone as Grace returned, a second folded paper in her hand.

"No," replied Grace. "I think it would be well for you to go with me. I don't know any one else I'd rather have," she added honestly.

"Thank you," bowed Elfreda, flushing and looking embarrassed at the compliment. "I'll never desert Micawber—Harlowe, I mean."

"Look serious. I am ready," said Grace softly. Then she knocked imperatively upon the door. There was a tense moment of waiting, then the door was opened by Kathleen West herself. Her sharp face looked still sharper as she eyed her visitors with ill-concealed disapproval.

"Good evening, Miss West," said Grace with distant politeness. "If you are not too busy, can you spare Miss Briggs and me a few moments? We have something of grave importance to say to you."

"Please make your business as brief as possible," snapped Kathleen, holding the door as though ready to close it in their faces the instant they stated their errand.

"Thank you," said Grace with unruffled calm. "We had better step inside your room, for a moment, at least. The hall is hardly the place for what I have to say."

The newspaper girl darted a swift, appraising glance at Grace. Her shrewd eyes fell before the steady light of Grace's gray ones. "Come in," she said shortly, then in a sarcastic tone, "Shall I close the door?"

"It would be better, I think," returned Grace in quietly significant tones.

The color flooded Kathleen West's sallow face. Her eyes began to flash ominously. "Your tone is insulting, Miss Harlowe!" she exclaimed.

"I answered your question, Miss West," returned Grace evenly. "However, I did not come here to quarrel with you. My errand has to do with the articles you write for the Sunday edition of your paper which you sign 'Elizabeth Vassar.' Miss Briggs has been following them for some time with a great deal of interest. This afternoon she found a part of what is evidently copy for an article."

Before Grace could go on Kathleen West had turned imperatively toward Elfreda. "Give it to me at once," she commanded. "I have hunted high and low for it. Your finding it is very strange, I must say. I am sure it was never off my desk."

Elfreda half closed her eyes and regarded the newspaper girl with the air of one viewing a rare curiosity for the first time. "Then your desk must be on the hall floor just outside the door," was her dry retort. "At least that is where I found this paper." A certain significant ring in the girl's voice admitted of no contradiction. For a brief interval no one spoke. Then Elfreda said smoothly, "As we appear to understand that point, go on, Grace."

"Give me my copy," reiterated Kathleen sullenly, before Grace had a chance to continue.

"Miss West," returned Grace very quietly, "Miss Briggs and I have read the copy which Miss Briggs found, and I have come here to say that you will be doing not only yourself but a great many other girls an injustice if you make public Miss Thayer's plans for the girls who remain at Overton for the holidays. Miss Thayer wishes the girls to feel perfectly independent in this matter, and whatever she contributes privately toward it is strictly her own affair. If this article appears on the school and college page, some of these girls are sure to hear of it and feel humiliated and resentful, particularly if the rest of the article is as callously cruel as its beginning."

Kathleen West laughed disagreeably. "That is not my affair. I have agreed to furnish my paper with snappy college news. This makes a good story. To supply my paper with good stories is my first business."

"Pardon me," retorted Grace scornfully, "I should imagine that loyalty to one's self and one's college constituted an Overton girl's first business."

"I can't see that this particular story has anything to do with being loyal to Overton," sneered Kathleen. "As for being loyal to myself, that is for me to judge. Who dares say I am disloyal?"

"Nothing very daring about that," drawled Elfreda. "I say so."

"You," stormed Kathleen. "Who are you?"

"J. Elfreda Briggs," murmured the stout girl sweetly.

"Yes," continued Kathleen sneeringly, "I have heard of the jumble you made of your freshman year. It took a number of influential friends to pull you into favor again, I believe."

"Not half such a jumble as you are making of yours," smiled Elfreda. Then she went on gravely: "I am glad you mentioned that freshman year. I did behave like an imbecile. Thanks to a number of girls who believed I was worth bothering with, I have learned to know what Overton requires of me. If you are wise, you'll face about, too. You will find it pays, and there are all sorts of pleasant compensations for what one expends in effort. That's all. I've said my say."

A curious, half-admiring expression flitted across Kathleen's thin little face. Then, turning to Grace, she said defiantly: "Give me my copy. I don't wish to rewrite it and I am going to send it to-night."

"I'm sorry you won't be fair about this, Miss West," said Grace regretfully, "but perhaps I can induce you to change your mind."

"I don't understand you," said Kathleen West stiffly.

Grace held a folded paper before the newspaper girl's eyes.

"Here is the Letter You Wrote the Dean."

"Here is the letter you wrote the dean regarding our bazaar. The dean gave it to me. She does not nor never will know who wrote it, unless you, yourself, tell her. That is something, however, that you and your conscience must decide. Here also is your page of copy. Under the circumstances, don't you think you might destroy this page and the others?"

Kathleen took the proffered papers with a set, enigmatic expression on her pointed features. Slowly she walked to her desk, picked up several sheets of copy and placing them with the sheet in her hand offered them to Grace.

Grace shook her head. "I will take your word," she said.

With a shrug of her shoulders the newspaper girl tore the papers across, then into bits, tossing them into her waste basket. "You win," she said with slangy effectiveness, then she added — "this time."

"Thank you," responded Grace gravely. "Good night, Miss West."

Kathleen did not respond.

Grace's hand was on the doorknob when the newspaper girl said harshly: "Wait. Don't think your lofty sentiments about college honor and all that nonsense impressed me to the point of destroying that copy. Once and for all I want you to understand that college ideals and traditions are not worrying me. I did not come to Overton to moon. I am only using college as a means to the end. What you offered me was a fair exchange. As you know a great deal too much about certain things, it is just as well to be on the safe side. I dare say I shall stumble on something else in the news line just as good as the charity dinner stunt." With a shrug of her shoulders that conveyed far more than words, she walked over to the window, turning her back directly upon her callers, nor did she change her position until an instant later the sound of the closing door announced to her that her unwelcome visitors had departed.

CHAPTER XVII

HIPPY LOOKS MYSTERIOUS

"Merry, Merry Christmas everywhere, Cheerily it ringeth through the air," sang Grace Harlowe joyously as she twined a long spray of ground pine about the chandelier in the hall, then stepping down from the stool on which she had been standing, backed off, viewing it critically.

"Oh, but it's good to be home!" she trilled, making a rush for her mother, who had just appeared in the door, and winding both arms tightly about her.

"My own little girl," returned her mother fondly. "How Father and I have missed you!"

"That's my greatest drawback to perfect happiness," sighed Grace, rubbing her soft cheek against her mother's: "Not to be able to be in two places at once. Now, if you were with me at Overton I wouldn't have a thing left to sigh for. You don't know how much I miss you, Mother, and Father, too. Sometimes I grow so homesick that I can't read or study or do anything but just think of you. Anne says she can always tell when I am extra blue."

"Your college life is only the beginning of our parting of ways, dear child. Mother would like to keep you safe and sheltered at home, but you are too active, too progressive, to be content as a home girl," said Mrs. Harlowe rather sadly. "You are likely to discover that your work lies far from Oakdale, but you know that whatever or wherever it may be your father and I will wish you Godspeed. You are to be perfectly free in the matter of choosing your future business of life."

"Don't I know that, you dearest, best mother a girl ever had!" exclaimed Grace, a quick mist clouding her gray eyes. "But never fear, I shan't ever stay away from you long at a time. I couldn't." Unwinding her arms from about her mother's neck, Grace linked one arm through Mrs. Harlowe's and marched her into the adjoining living room.

"Doesn't it look exactly like Christmas?" she asked proudly. "See the tree. Isn't it a beauty? We have loads of presents, too. Isn't Miriam a goose and a dear all rolled into one? She won't come to my Christmas tree because she isn't one of the Eight Originals. I asked her to be a Ninth Original, but she said 'No.' She is coming, though, only she doesn't know it. David received a telegram from Arnold Evans yesterday. He is expected to-night on the six o'clock train. Miriam doesn't know that, either. She thinks he was unable to come, and won't she be surprised when he appears to escort her to our house?" Grace laughed gleefully in anticipation of Miriam's astonishment at sight of Arnold Evans, who was always a welcome addition to their little company.

Two immeasurably happy days had passed since the train from the east had steamed away from Oakdale, leaving three eager girls on the platform of the station. The evening train had brought Eva Allen, Marian Barber, Jessica Bright and Nora O'Malley. Grace, Miriam and Anne, accompanied by a slender, brown-eyed young woman, whom they addressed as Mabel, had met the train. Jessica Bright's radiant delight at beholding the face of her foster sister, Mabel Allison, can be better imagined than described. Mabel and her mother had arrived three days before, and were to divide their month's stay in Oakdale between the Gibsons of Hawk's Nest, an estate several miles from Oakdale, and the Brights. Jessica's aunt, Mr. Bright's only sister, who had never married, now presided over the Bright household, with a grace and hospitality that gained for her not only the reputation of a delightful hostess, but the adoration of Jessica's friends as well.

It was now the day before Christmas, and that evening Grace had invited her dearest friends to help her keep Christmas Eve.

"Just as though we could get along without Miriam!" she exclaimed enthusiastically. "You haven't any idea, Mother, what a power for good she is at Overton. It isn't half so much what she says as the way she says it. She has so much tact. Elfreda worships her."

"I am sorry Elfreda could not come home with you," commented Mrs. Harlowe.

"We were all sorry," returned Grace regretfully. "She may run down for a day before we go back to college. We have promised her a winter picnic in Upton Wood and a supper at old Jean's if she comes. That ought to tempt her. Oh, there's the bell. I know that is Anne! She promised to be here early. The Eight Originals are going to trim the tree, you know."

Grace rushed to the front door to open it for Anne, who staggered into the hall, her arms full of packages. "Oh, catch them," she gasped. "I'm going to drop them all and two of them are breakable."

Grace sprang forward to relieve Anne of her load. One fat package fell to the floor and rolled under the living-room sofa. Grace made a laughing dive after it. Then, dropping to her knees, peered under the sofa, dragged it forth in triumph and presented it to Anne.

Anne thanked her. "It is for Hippy," she smiled. "You might know that it would behave in an extraordinary manner. I've been so busy this morning. I was up before seven, helped Mother with the breakfast, went on a shopping expedition, and now I'm here. It isn't eleven o'clock yet, either."

"Imagine Everett Southard's leading woman washing dishes," smiled Grace.

"She did, though," rejoined Anne cheerfully, "and swept the dining room and kitchen, too. I have an invitation to deliver. I am going to entertain the Eight Originals and Mrs. Gray at my house next Tuesday evening. You'll receive a real summons to my party by mail."

"How formal," said Grace gayly. "However, Miss Harlowe accepts with pleasure Miss Pierson's kind invitation, etc."

"Miss Pierson is duly honored by Miss Harlowe's prompt acceptance," laughed Anne. "Do the boys know about bringing their presents here?"

"Oh, yes," returned Grace. "There goes the door bell!" She hurried to the door, flinging it wide open to admit three stalwart young men whose clean-cut, boyish faces shone with good humor.

"Hurrah for old Kris Kringle!" cried Hippy, who was in the lead, as he skipped nimbly into the living-room, and set down the heavy suit case he carried with a flourish. Then backing into David Nesbit, who stood directly behind him, he said apologetically: "I beg your pardon, David, but if you will insist in taking up so much space you must expect to have your toes trampled upon."

"I don't take up one half as much space as you do," flung back David.

"True; I hadn't looked at the matter in that light," Hippy agreed hastily. "Let us change the subject. I am so pleased, Grace, to know that you are giving this little affair in my honor. I really didn't expect to——"

"Be put out of the house," finished Reddy with a menacing step toward Hippy.

"Exactly," agreed Hippy. "No, I don't mean that at all. I was about to say that I really didn't expect to be obliged to put Reddy Brooks out of the house for threatened assault. It seems too bad to mar the gentle peace of Christmas by such deeds of violence." Hippy sighed loudly, then with a gesture of finality warily sidled toward Reddy, an expression of deadly determination on his round face. The sound of a ringing laugh from the doorway caused him to forget his grievance and make for the door as fast as his legs would carry him. "Reddy, you are saved," he announced, leading Nora O'Malley into the room. "Thank your gentle preserver, Miss O'Malley."

"You mean you are saved," corrected Reddy with a derisive grin.

"All the same, all the same," retorted Hippy airily. "I am saved because you are saved, and you are saved because I am saved. We are both saved this time, aren't we, Grace?"

"Yes, I forbid either one of you to usher the other out," laughed Grace.

"There, Reddy, you heard!" exclaimed Hippy. "Now heed."

"Have you seen Jessica this morning, Nora?" asked Reddy, answering Hippy's admonition with a withering look.

"She will be here later," replied Nora. "She has gone shopping with Mabel, who is going to Hawk's Nest for Christmas Eve."

"We are all booked for Christmas Day with our families," smiled David.

"Thank goodness we have them," said Hippy with a seriousness that surprised even himself.

"Same here, Hippy," agreed David gravely.

"And here," was the united response from the others.

Jessica, who had seen Mabel Allison into the car Mrs. Gibson had sent to convey her to Hawk's Nest, was the next arrival. Later Tom Gray appeared with a grip and a suit case. When the real work of trimming the tree began, Hippy retired to the library table with the plea that he had not yet tagged his gifts. To that end he wrote what seemed to Nora O'Malley, who eyed him suspiciously, a surprising amount of cards, chuckling softly to himself as he wrote. Happening to catch her eye he looked rather guilty, then, cocking his head to one side, simpered languishingly, "What shall I say to thee, heart of my heart?" Nora's tip-tilted little nose was promptly elevated still higher, and she walked away without observing the triumphant gleam in Hippy's blue eyes.

At one o'clock the Eight Originals halted for luncheon, which proved to be a merry meal. By half-past two o'clock the tall balsam tree, heavy with its weight of decorations and strange Christmas fruit, was pronounced finished, and the party of jubilant young people reluctantly separated to assemble after dinner for one of their old-time frolics.

The evening train brought Arnold Evans, and Miriam found herself whisked down Chapel Hill toward Grace's home by David and Arnold despite her protests that neither she nor Arnold really belonged. "You and Arnold are the honorary members," David reminded her, "and are, therefore, eligible to all our revels."

When, at eight o'clock, the little group of guests, which included Mrs. Gray, had gathered in the Harlowe's cozy living room and to Mr. Harlowe had fallen the honor of playing Santa Claus, something peculiar happened. Nearly all the gifts fell to Hippy, who rose with every repetition of his name, bowed profoundly, grinned significantly in his best Chessy-cat manner and, swooping down upon the gifts, gathered them unto himself. As he was about to take smiling possession of a large, flat package an indignant, "Let me see that package, Mr. Harlowe," from Nora O'Malley caused all eyes to be focused upon it.

"Just as I suspected," sputtered Nora, glaring at the offending Hippy, whose grin appeared to grow wider with every second. Taking the package from Mr. Harlowe, she triumphantly held up a holly-wreathed card that had been deftly concealed beneath a fold of tissue paper, and read, "To Grace, with love from Nora."

"Discovered!" exclaimed Hippy in hollow tones, making a dive for the package and failing to secure it.

Nora held it above her head. "Here, Grace, it's yours," she explained. "Don't pay any attention to that other card."

Grace had turned her attention to a large tag that was fastened to the holly ribbon with which the package was tied. She read aloud, "To my esteemed friend, Hippy, from his humble little admirer, Nora O'Malley."

The instant of silence was followed by a shout of laughter, in which Nora joined. "You rascal!" she exclaimed, shaking her finger at Hippy. "I knew you were planning mischief when you sat over there writing those cards. Take all those presents, girls. I am sure they don't belong to this deceitful reprobate."

Hippy at once set up a dismal wail, and clutched his packages to his breast, dropping all but two in the process. These were snapped up by Reddy and Nora almost before they touched the floor.

"Here's the umbrella I thought I bought for Tom," growled Reddy, as he ripped off the simple inscription, "To Hippy, with love, Reddy."

"Yes, and here is the monogrammed stationery I ordered made for Jessica," added Nora, glaring at the stout young man, who smiled blithely in return as one who had received an especial favor.

"You are holding on to two of my presents, though," he reminded.

Nora made a hasty inspection of the packages, then shoved the two presents toward him. "There they are," she said severely. "If I had known how badly you were going to behave, I wouldn't have given you a thing."

"Take your scarf pin, Indian giver," jeered Hippy, holding out a small package, then jerking it back again.

"How do you know it's a scarf pin?" inquired Nora.

"My intuition tells me, my child," returned Hippy gently.

"Then your intuition is all wrong," declared Nora O'Malley disdainfully.

"Always ready to argue," sighed Hippy.

"Mrs. Gray, I appeal to you, don't allow Hippy and Nora to start an argument. There won't be either time or chance for anything else."

"Hippy and Nora, be good children," laughingly admonished the sprightly old lady.

"Look out for Hippy's cards," David cautioned Mr. Harlowe.

The rest of the gifts were distributed without accident, and then by common consent a great unwrapping began, accompanied by rapturous "ohs," and plenty of "thank yous."

It was almost one o'clock on Christmas morning before any of the guests even thought of home. After the tree had been despoiled of its bloom, an impromptu show followed in which the young folks performed the stunts for which they were famous. Then came supper, dancing, and the usual Virginia Reel, led by Mr. Harlowe and Mrs. Gray, in which Hippy distinguished himself by a series of quaint and marvelous steps.

"One more good time to add to our dozens of others," said Miriam Nesbit softly as she kissed Grace good night. "I feel to-night as though I could say with particular emphasis: 'Peace on Earth, Good Will Toward Men.'"

"And I feel," said Hippy, who had overheard Miriam's low-toned remark, "as though I had been unjustly and unkindly treated. I was cheated of over half my Christmas gifts by those unblushing miscreants known as David Nesbit, Reddy Brooks and Tom Gray. Nora O'Malley helped them, too."

"Jessica and Reddy, will you take me home to-night?" asked Nora sweetly, edging away from the complaining Hippy.

"We shall be only too pleased to be your escort," Reddy answered with alacrity, casting a sidelong glance of triumph at Hippy.

"And I shall be only too pleased to annihilate Reddy Brooks for daring to suggest any such thing," retorted Hippy, striding toward the offending Reddy.

"Come, come, Hippy," laughed Mrs. Harlowe, who enjoyed Hippy's pranks as much as did his companions, "this is Christmas, you know. Why not let Reddy live?"

"Very well, I will," agreed Hippy, "but only to please you, Mrs. Harlowe. Once we leave here, the annihilation process is likely to begin at the first disrespectful word on the part of a certain crimson-haired individual whose name I won't mention. It will be a painful process."

"There isn't the slightest doubt about it being painful to you," was Reddy's grim retort.

"I wonder if I had better wait until after Christmas to do the deed," mused Hippy. "There's Reddy's family to consider. Perhaps I had better—"

"—behave yourself in future and not refer to your friends as 'miscreants' after appropriating their Christmas presents," lectured David Nesbit.

"All right, I agree to your proposition on one condition," stipulated Hippy.

"Something to eat, I suppose," said David wearily.

"No; you are a wild guesser as well as a slanderer. If Nora O'Malley will withdraw the cruel request she just made I will forgive even Reddy."

And when the little party of young folks started on their homeward way the forgiving Hippy with Nora O'Malley on his arm marched gayly along behind the forgiven, but wholly unappreciative Reddy.

CHAPTER XVIII

OLD JEAN'S STORY

"It's 'Ho for the forest!'" sang Tom Gray jubilantly, as he waved his stout walking stick over the low stone wall that separated the party of picnickers from Upton Wood.

"Isn't it magnificent?" asked Grace of Anne, her gray eyes glowing as she looked ahead at the snowy road that stretched like a great white ribbon between the deep green rows of pine and fir trees.

"Perfect," agreed Anne dreamily, who was drinking in the solemn beauty of the snow-wrapped forest, an expression of reverence on her small face.

"I wonder if the snow in the road is very deep?" soliloquized Jessica unsentimentally.

"How can you break in upon our rapt musings with such commonplaces?" laughed Grace. "To return to earth; I don't imagine the snow is deep. This road is much traveled, and the snow looks fairly well packed. What do you say, Huntsman Gray?" She turned to Tom with a smile.

"It isn't deep. All aboard for Upton Wood!" called Tom cheerily. "Come on, Grace." He extended a helping hand to her.

But Grace needed no assistance. With a laughing shake of her head she vaulted the low wall as easily as Tom himself could have cleared it. Nora followed her, then Miriam, while Anne and Jessica were content to allow themselves to be assisted by David and Reddy. Then the picnickers swung into the wide snow-packed road that wound its way to the other end of Upton Wood, a matter of perhaps ten miles. Being a part of the road to the state capital and a famous automobile route it was sedulously looked after and kept in good condition, and was therefore not difficult to travel.

The cabin of old Jean, the hunter, was situated some distance from the main road in the thickest part of the forest. The day before, the five young men, with a bobsled filled with grocers' supplies, had driven to the point of the road nearest the cabin and a brisk unloading had followed. After their first trip to the cottage old Jean had returned to the sleigh with them, his fur cap awry, gesticulating delightedly and chattering volubly as he walked. Of a surety Mamselle Grace and her friends were welcome. He deplored the fact that they had insisted upon bringing their own provisions, but David, who suspected the old hunter's larder to be none too well stocked with eatables, had quieted Jean's remonstrances with the diplomatic assertion that the affair having been planned by the "Eight Originals Plus Two," as they had now agreed to call themselves, and given in honor of the old hunter himself, it was their privilege to pay the piper. Jean had shaken his head rather dubiously over the miscellaneous heap of groceries that spread over at least a quarter of his floor, but his first protest had been laughingly silenced by the five sturdy foresters, who threatened to turn him out of house and home if he did not allow his friends to celebrate in peace.

On this particular morning Jean had been up and doing since five o'clock. He had decorated his cabin walls with ground pine and evergreen, and as a last touch had, with many chuckles, suspended from the ceiling an unusually perfect piece of mistletoe, which he had tramped into Oakdale early that morning to secure. He had cleaned his rifle first, then swept and scrubbed his cabin floor, and the pine table off which he ate, until the most critical housekeeper could have found no fault with the shining cleanliness of the place. The rousing fire that he built in the big fireplace soon dried the floor, and after arranging his few household effects to the best advantage, Jean busied himself with getting in a good supply of wood before his young guests, who had set the hour of three o'clock for their arrival, should appear upon the scene.

It was precisely ten minutes to three when the little company reached the top of the hill at the foot of which nestled old Jean's cottage, and halted for a moment before descending.

"Sound the call of the Elf's Horn, Tom," demanded Grace. "I only wish I could sound it. I've tried over and over again, but I can't do it."

"It is a gift which the fairies reserve for only a few favored mortals," teased Tom.

"Then I am not one of them," declared Grace. "I have watched for fairies since I was a little girl and never met with one yet. I know every individual fairy in Grimms', Andersen's and Lang's by reputation, too."

"What about your fairy prince?" was Tom's quick question. The two pairs of gray eyes met. Grace smiled with frank amusement.

"I have never looked for a fairy prince," she said lightly. "I never cared half so much about the fairy princes and the clothes and weddings as I did about giants, witches and spells, mysterious happenings and magic mirrors. I loved 'The Brave Little Tailor' and 'The Youth Who Could Not Shiver and Shake.'"

"I always liked the 'False Bride' and 'Rapunzel,'" remarked Jessica sentimentally, who had come up beside Grace and Tom.

"Of what are you talking?" asked Nora, who had caught Jessica's last word.

"We were naming the fairy tales we always liked best."

"I always liked the 'Magic Fiddle,'" said Nora, with a reminiscent chuckle. "I used to keep a copy of Grimms' Fairy Tales in my desk at school, just for that story. It always made me giggle. I could fairly see all those poor people dancing whether they wished to dance or not. Ask Hippy what his favorite fairy tale is," she dimpled, lowering her voice.

"Say, Hippopotamus," called Tom, "what's your favorite fairy tale?" Hippy, who stood a little to one side, appeared to think deeply, then said with a sentimental smile: "The 'Table Prepare Thyself' story. Oh, if I might have had such a table!" Hippy sighed dolefully. "Then I would never have been obliged when out on these excursions to humbly beg for crumbs to sustain my failing strength till such time as you slow-pokes saw fit to eat."

"Don't I always give you things to eat when everyone else laughs at you?" demanded Nora belligerently.

"Yes, my noble benefactor," whined Hippy, "but you didn't to-day."

"I don't intend to, either," was Nora's unfeeling response. "I purposely told Tom to ask you that. I knew you'd name one that had a good deal about eating in it."

"Stop squabbling," commanded Reddy, his fingers fastened in the back of Hippy's collar, "or down the hill you go. Keep quiet, now, Tom is going to perform."

Tom placed his hands to his mouth. His friends listened intently. Then came the peculiar whistle that sounded like the note of a trumpet. Tom whistled repeatedly, and two minutes later they saw old Jean come racing up the steep path toward them. He had heard the mysterious Elf's Horn.

"Never forgot it, did you, Jean?" laughed Tom, seizing the old man's hand and shaking it warmly.

"No, Monsieur Tom; once I hear, it is impossible that I should forget," replied Jean in his quaint English. "An' now that you have honor me this afternoon, it is well that you come to my cabin where the fire burn for you an' the coffee wait, an' all is ready for my frien's who mak' so long walk for the sake of ol' Jean."

"Of course we did, Jean," smiled Grace as they started for the cabin. "Don't we always come to see you when we are home from college?"

"It is true, Mamselle Grace," returned Jean solemnly. "I am lucky man to have such fren's."

"Don't look so sad over it, Jean!" exclaimed Hippy. "Be merry, and gayly dance as I do." He essayed several fantastic steps over the frozen ground, stubbed his toe on a projecting root and lunged forward, falling heavily into a huge snowdrift, his hands and face plowing into the snow.

"Ha, ha!" jeered Reddy. "'Be merry, and gayly dance as I do.' No, thank you. I prefer to walk along like an ordinary human being."

"That is exactly what you are," was Hippy's calm retort from the snowdrift, "'an ordinary human being.'" Floundering out of the drift he shook himself free of snow and, undaunted by his fall, went on skipping and pirouetting toward the cabin, while his companions shrieked mirthful comments into his apparently unhearing ears.

How fast the afternoon and evening slipped away! The girls insisted on helping Jean with the dinner, and at half-past five the whole party sat down at the rude table that had been improvised by the boys the day before. Eating in the heart of the forest made things taste infinitely better than at home. Never before had there been such coffee, or steak, or baked potatoes! There was dessert, too—Mrs. Nesbit's famous fruit cake and Mrs. Harlowe's equally prized mince pie, besides fruit and nuts, Jean adding the latter to the feast. Then everyone's health was drunk in grape juice, and it was almost seven o'clock before Jean and his guests rose from the table.

"Ten minutes to seven," declared David, consulting his watch. "We must leave here at eight o'clock. We ought to be home by nine. I feel very responsible for these youngsters, Jean. It was I who agreed to play chaperon."

"Youngsters, indeed," growled Reddy scornfully. "Listen to Methuselah."

"Tell us a story before we go, Jean," begged Grace. She loved to hear the old hunter tell in his quaint way of his many perilous adventures in the great northwestern woods of Canada, where he had spent so many years of his life.

"If Mamselle Grace like I will tell of w'en I track the fierce panther who have kill my lambs, an' what happen to me."

"Oh, splendid!" cried Grace. "We should love to hear it."

The glow from the big back log reflected the interested faces of the others. Jean's stories were always well received. Settling himself cross-legged on the floor, his back against the wall, he related how, after tracking a panther all day, he had slipped while going down a steep bank and losing his footing had plunged to the bottom. How he had lain there bruised and helpless with a broken leg, expecting at any time to see the beast he had been tracking bear down upon him. How at last, after hours of unspeakable agony, help had come in the shape of a tall, strongly built young man, whose cabin was not far off and who had carried Jean to it, then, after roughly setting the injured leg, and making his patient as comfortable as might be expected under the circumstances, he had ridden thirty miles for a doctor, then tended the old hunter until his leg healed.

"Ten week I stay in bed an' this good frien' take care of me. He inten' to go to Alaska for gold. He say he have wife once an' baby but they die in railroad wreck. He never see their bodies. He very sad. The fire in the train burn everybody, all t'ings." Jean waved his arms comprehensively. "He stay by me until I am well. Then he say, 'Jean, come along to Alaska.' But I say, 'No. I am too ol'. I wish live all my days in Canada woods.' So he go on. After many years he write. Only last summer I have receive his letter. He have found plenty gold, an' is rich. He say when he come back, then he will buy for me a new rifle an' give me much money. But what does Jean care for money? Rather I would see my frien' whose letter I have always keep."

The old man ceased speaking and looked retrospectively into the fire. Then, without speaking, he rose, shuffled to a small table in one corner of the room, and opening the drawer took from it a well-thumbed envelope. Returning to the group he handed it to Grace, saying proudly: "This is the letter my frien' write. Will Mamselle Grace read?"

Grace obediently took the letter from the envelope.

"My dear Jean:" she read. "How can I ever forgive myself for neglecting you so long? I can only say that though I have failed to make good my promise to write, you have never been forgotten by me. Jean, I am sorry you didn't come here with me. I found gold, more than I can spend in a lifetime, and I have made you a stockholder in my mine. I am coming back to the States next spring and will look you up first of all. I am sending this to the old address, trusting that if you are not there it will be forwarded to you. I used to think it would be glorious to be rich, but now that I am alone in the world, money seems a poor substitute for my lost happiness.

"Let me hear from you soon, Jean, and address your letter, Post Office Box 462, Nome, Alaska. I hope you are well and happy. You always were a sunshiny old chap. Here's hoping.

> "Your old friend,
> "D<small>ENTON</small>."

"Is it not a very gran' letter?" asked old Jean with anxious pride. "My frien' Denton have study in college, too."

"Indeed it is, Jean," agreed Anne warmly.

"Your friend seems to be the right sort of comrade, even if he is a bad correspondent," remarked David Nesbit.

"Something like me," murmured Hippy gently.

No one appeared to notice this modest assertion.

"Sounds like a page from a best seller, doesn't it, Grace?" asked Tom laughingly.

Grace did not answer. She was gazing at the signature of the letter with perplexed eyes. She was wondering why the name Denton seemed so familiar. Remembrance came suddenly—Ruth, of course. With that recollection came a sudden startling train of thought. Ruth's father had gone west, had been heard from in Nevada, then disappeared. Jean's friend had lost his wife and child on a westbound train. Here, however, Grace's supposition proved weak. Both wife and child had been burned to death in the railroad wreck. Still, mistakes in identification were frequently made on such painful occasions. Grace went back to her first supposition. "It is the only shred of a clew that I have run across yet," she reflected. "I am going to hang to it and see where it leads. And to think that perhaps old Jean once knew Ruth's father. It's unbelievable."

"We must start in ten minutes." David's crisp, business-like tones brought her to a realization of her immediate surroundings.

"Ten minutes is long enough for me to say what is on my mind," Grace said eagerly. Then she began to tell of Ruth, her poverty, and her great wish to know whether her father were dead or alive.

Knowing Grace as they did, her friends guessed that she had something of real importance to impart. When she came to the part about Ruth's father going west after promising to send for his little family, a light began to dawn upon them, and Jessica exclaimed: "Why, they must have been killed while on their way to join him!"

"It is so. Mamselle speak the truth!" almost shouted Jean. "It was then they die. He have tol' me so many times."

"Then the man who saved Jean must have been Ruth's father!" exclaimed Miriam, "and a dreadful mistake was made in telling him his child was dead, too. The packet fastened by a cord about Ruth's neck ought easily to have proved her identity. Perhaps the packet was stolen."

"Then how did Ruth come by the watch and letter?" asked Grace.

"I give it up," replied Miriam. "It certainly is a tangled web."

"But we shall straighten it," said Grace resolutely. "The next thing to do is to find Mr. Denton. Tell me, Jean, how many years since you first met Mr. Denton?"

Jean counted laboriously on his fingers. "Twelve years," he finally announced, "an' say his family have died six years then."

"Eighteen years," mused Grace, "and Ruth is twenty-two. The years seem to tally with the rest of the story, too. Will you give me Mr. Denton's address and allow me to write to him, Jean?"

"Whatever Mamselle Grace wishes shall be hers," averred Jean.

"Then I'll write the letter to-morrow. The sooner it is written and sent, the sooner we shall receive an answer to it," declared Grace. "That is unless he is dead. But I have a strange presentiment that he is alive. What do you think, Jean?" she turned to the old hunter, who nodded sagely.

"I think my frien', he alive, too," agreed Jean, "an' I hope, mebbe I shall see again."

"You shall see him and so shall Ruth, if letters can accomplish your wish, Jean," promised Grace.

"Eight o'clock," announced David judicially.

No one paid the slightest attention to him, however, Ruth Denton's affairs being altogether too engrossing a matter for discussion. It was half-past eight when, after a hearty vote of thanks and three cheers for old Jean, the picnickers climbed the little hill and took the moonlit homeward trail.

CHAPTER XIX

TELLING RUTH THE NEWS

"Yes, it was a busy two weeks," declared Arline Thayer, "and yet, oh, Grace, you can't possibly know how slowly the time has gone. I am sure I could live all the rest of my life on a desert island if I had the Semper Fidelis crowd with me. Of course, Ruth helped a whole lot, but you know Ruth isn't a butterfly like I am. She has had so many cares and disappointments that she isn't as gay in her wildest moments as I am in my ordinary ones. Besides, it was so hard to be sure that I was doing and saying the right thing. I was so afraid of hurting some one's feelings, or of being accused of trying to patronize those girls.

"The dinner passed off beautifully. Every girl who stayed over was there. It cost me most of my check." Here Arline smiled rather ruefully. "But you never saw so many happy girls. Many of them had never been to either Martell's or Vinton's for dinner. I was at Vinton's and Ruth was at Martell's. No one had the slightest idea that there was anything cut and dried. We did all the other stunts; the play and the masquerade, and I am so tired." Arline curled herself up on Grace's couch, looking like an exhausted kitten. "I wonder if Elfreda has any tea," she said plaintively.

"Of course she has," smiled Grace. "So have I. I'll make you some at once. Then I have something perfectly amazing to tell you. You won't remember whether you are tired or not after you hear my news."

Taking the little copper tea-kettle, Grace went for water, leaving Arline considerably mystified and mildly excited. When at last the tea was ready, and Grace had placed crackers, nabisco wafers and a plate of home-made nut cookies on the table between them, Arline said impatiently, "Do begin."

"Daffydowndilly, this is the strangest news you ever heard. Ready?"

"Ready," echoed Arline.

"We believe Ruth's father is still living and in Alaska."

There was a little cry of rapture from Arline as she hastily set down her cup and caught Grace's hand in hers. "Congratulations," she trilled. "I knew you'd find him. I've seen it in your eye for months."

"Nonsense," laughed Grace, "I don't deserve a particle of credit. It was quite by accident that I learned what I know of him." Thereupon an account of their visit to old Jean followed, and Arline was soon in full possession of the details.

"Shall you tell Ruth?" was her first question after Grace had finished.

"What would you do?" Grace asked.

"I don't think it would be best to tell her yet," returned Arline slowly. "Suppose we were to find that he had died or disappeared again since your old hunter received his letter. Think how dreadful that would be after telling her that he was alive and well. We must not arouse her hopes until we know."

Grace nodded gravely. "That is what I thought. I am glad you are of the same mind. No one here except yourself and Elfreda have been told. Of course, Anne and Miriam heard it at the same time I did. I wrote to Mr. Denton at once, but I suppose my letter isn't more than half way to Nome yet."

"Oh, it is the greatest thing that ever happened," exulted Arline. "Ruth's father found at last, away up in old, cold Alaska. Hurrah!"

"Stop making so much noise," cautioned Grace, "while I tell you what I propose doing. It is two weeks since I wrote to Mr. Denton. I am going to write another letter to him before long. If he doesn't answer that, I shall stop for a while, then write again. If he is not in Nome I shall request the post-master to forward the letters, if possible."

At this juncture a knock sounded on the almost closed door, then Elfreda came hurrying in, her cheeks glowing from her walk in the January wind. "Were you talking secrets?" she demanded, without stopping to greet Arline.

"She was Standing Close to the Door."

"No,—that is—yes," replied Arline. "Grace was telling me about Ruth's father and—"

Elfreda dropped on the couch beside Arline with a groan of dismay. "Why didn't you close the door?" she asked gloomily.

"Why? What has happened?" questioned Grace anxiously.

"Nothing much," retorted Elfreda, "only that West person was standing as close to your door as she could possibly stand without attracting marked attention. She was listening, too. I saw her when I reached the first landing. At first I thought I would walk up to her and call her to account for eavesdropping. But before I could make up my mind just what to do she went on down the hall to her room. I suppose you will hear about this affair of Ruth finding her father from a dozen different sources to-morrow. She will go directly to the Wicks-Hampton faction with the news. She may have gone already."

"This is dreadful," gasped Grace in consternation, "but our own fault. Will I ever learn to keep my door closed and either whisper my secrets or else lock them behind my lips?"

"It was my fault," declared Arline contritely. "I was shouting, 'Ruth's father found at last!' at the top of my voice. Grace told me to subside."

"Perhaps she only heard that much," comforted Elfreda, trying to be a little more hopeful.

"Suppose she tells Ruth," suggested Arline nervously.

Grace's eyes met those of her friend's in genuine alarm. Without a word she went to the closet and reaching for her coat and furs slipped them on. Jamming her fur cap down on her head, she pinned it securely, thrust her hands into her muff and walked to the door. "Elfreda, you will take care of Arline, won't you? She is going to stay with me for dinner. I am going to Ruth's and I think perhaps I had better go alone. I'll be back as soon as possible, and bring Ruth with me, if I can. Tell Mrs. Elwood that Ruth will be here. I must be off. I will see you at dinner."

Grace was out of the room and down the stairs in a twinkling. As she set off toward Ruth's at a rapid pace she wondered if there was not some way in which she might capitulate with this strange girl who seemed so determined to blot the pages of her freshman year with unworthy deeds. "I am so disappointed," Grace reflected. "I did wish to like her because she was Mabel's friend, but she is so—so—different." It cost Grace an effort to end her sentence mildly. "But I'm not going to gossip about her, even to myself."

After ringing three times Ruth's tired-eyed landlady opened the door to Grace with a mumbled apology about being in the attic when the bell rang. Grace hurried up the two flights of stairs and down the long, bare hall to Ruth's room. She paused an instant before knocking, half expecting to hear the sound of voices inside. All was still. Grace knocked twice, pausing between knocks. It was a signal Ruth and her intimate friends had adopted.

Ruth answered the signal, a book in her hand. She gave a little cry of delight at seeing Grace. "How funny! I was just thinking of you. Come in and take off your wraps. Did you come to help me cook supper? You promised me you would some day."

"No; I came to take you back to Wayne Hall with me. But, first of all, has Kathleen West been here to see you within the past half hour?" said Grace, stepping into the room and closing the door after her.

"No," replied Ruth wonderingly. "Why do you ask? But do sit down, Grace."

"I'm so glad," sighed Grace, sitting on the edge of the chair, "because she overheard something that I wish to tell you first."

"I don't understand," was Ruth's perplexed answer.

"I don't blame you for not understanding," smiled Grace. Then she rose, and, crossing the room, put her hands on her friend's shoulder. "Ruth," she said gently, "if you might have one wish granted to you, what would you wish?"

"To find my father," was the instant reply.

"That is what I thought you would say," returned Grace quietly. "Can you bear good news?"

"Yes." Ruth's face had turned very white. She pulled one of Grace's hands from her shoulder, holding it in hers. "Tell me," she whispered tensely.

Grace's gray eyes filled with tears. The hungry look in Ruth's eyes told its own story. "He is alive, Ruth," she said, steadying her voice. "At least he was alive less than six months ago. I'll begin at the very first and tell you everything."

It was half an hour later when the two friends set out for Wayne Hall.

"I am so happy; it seems as though I must be with you girls to-night," declared Ruth. "I am so anxious to see Arline. My Daffydowndilly will be happy, too, for my sake. And Grace, I have a strange presentiment that I shall see him before long. I can't think of him as anything but alive. I'm so glad that you told me. It would have been a dreadful shock to have had the news come through Miss West or her friends."

"She hasn't the slightest idea that we know she was in the hall," said Grace. "I imagine you will hear of your father through half a dozen different sources in the morning. I don't believe she intended to tell you to-day. I think it was part of her plan to take you by surprise and completely unnerve you. Alberta Wicks and Mary Hampton are efficient town criers," Grace added bitterly. "She depended on them to spread the news in the cruelest way."

"Why, Grace, I never heard you speak so bitterly of any one before!" exclaimed Ruth.

"Ruth, to tell the honest truth, I am thoroughly disgusted with those two girls," confessed Grace wearily. "They have been at the bottom of every annoyance I have had since I came to Overton. It may not be charitable to say so, but I shall certainly not regret seeing them graduated and gone from Overton. I know it sounds selfish, but I can't help it. I mean it. And now we are going to talk only of delightful things. I think we ought to give a spread to-night in honor of you. It isn't every day one finds a long-lost father. Arline is going to stay to dinner, and, of course, she'll stay afterward."

Grace's proposal of a spread met with gleeful approval, and in spite of a hearty six-o'clock dinner, there was no lack of appetite when at ten o'clock Elfreda, who insisted on taking the labor of the spread upon her own shoulders, appeared in the door announcing that it was ready. By borrowing Grace's table and using it in conjunction with her own, employing the bureau scarf for a centerpiece, and filling up the bare spaces with paper napkins, the table assumed the dignity of a banqueting board. There were even glasses and plates and spoons enough to go round and one could have either grape juice or tea, Elfreda informed them. "You'd better take tea first, though, because there are only two bottles of grape juice, and we need that for the toast to Ruth's father. Of course if you insist upon having grape juice——"

"Tea," was the judiciously lowered chorus from the obliging guests.

"Thank you," bowed Elfreda. "I wouldn't have given you the grape juice, at any rate."

By half-past ten nothing remained of the feast but the grape juice, and the guests began clamoring insistently for that.

"We are breaking the ten-thirty rule into microscopic pieces," declared Elfreda as she dropped slices of orange and pineapple on the ice in the bottom of the glasses, added orange juice, sugar and grape juice. "If it isn't sweet enough, help yourself to sugar. The bowl is on the table. And you can only have one straw apiece. The commissary department is short on straws. A word of warning, don't drink the toast to Ruth's father through a straw," she ended with a giggle.

The giggle proved infectious and went the round of the table. Grace was the first to remember the toast to be drunk. Elfreda had just poured the sixth, her own glass of grape juice, and slipped into her place at the table. Rising to her feet Grace said simply, "To Ruth's father. May she see him soon." The toast was drunk standing. Ruth still looked rather dazed. She could not yet think of her father as a reality.

"I thank you all," she said tremulously, her eyes misty. "Of course you know I am not quite certain of my great happiness, but I am going to write to Father to-morrow, and perhaps before long I'll have a letter to show you."

"If Ruth is to be surprised now, some one will have to get up early in the morning," declared Elfreda with satisfaction, as she collected the dishes for washing after the guests had departed.

"And that some one will be doomed to feel foolish," added Miriam.

CHAPTER XX

ELFREDA REALIZES HER AMBITION

Midyears, a season of terror to freshmen, a still alarming period to sophomores, but no very great bugbear to the two upper classes, came and went. During that strenuous week the usual amount of midnight oil was burnt, the usual amount of feverish reviewing done, and the usual amount of celebrating indulged in when the ordeal was passed.

"Don't forget the game to-morrow," said J. Elfreda Briggs to the girls at her end of the breakfast table one morning in early March. "The only one this year in which the celebrated center, Miss Josephine Elfreda Briggs, will take part. Sounds like a grand opera announcement, doesn't it? Maybe it hasn't taken endless energy to keep that team together and up to the mark. But our captain is a hustler and we are marvels," she added modestly.

"I need no bard to sing my praises," began Miriam mischievously.

"I didn't say 'I,'" retorted Elfreda. "I said 'we.'"

"Meaning 'I'," interposed Emma Dean wickedly.

"As you like," flung back Elfreda sweetly. "You needn't come to the game, you know, if you think it is to be a one-player affair."

"Oh, I'll be there, never fear," Emma assured her. "I have a special banner of junior blue to wear."

Only one color had been chosen by 19— for their junior year, one of the new shades of blue which Gertrude Wells had at once renamed "junior" blue. It was greatly affected by the juniors for ties, belts, hat trimmings and girdles.

"Doesn't it seem strange not to be on the team this year, Miriam?" asked Grace. "That is, when one stops to think about it. It never occurred to me until this moment how much I have missed basketball. Mabel Ashe said that we'd just simply drift away from it this year, and so we have. Now we are going to cheer Elfreda on to victory."

"Elfreda is an artist in making baskets," commended Miriam.

"Much obliged," rejoined Elfreda, "but your praise doesn't turn my head in the least. You can judge better of my artistic qualities after the game."

"We hope to secure seats in the gallery," said Anne. "The front ones, of course, are reserved for the faculty, but if we go to the gym very early we may get good seats."

"I am not going to wait for you, if you don't mind, Miriam," remarked Elfreda, rising. "I must see our captain before going to chapel this morning."

"Run along," said Miriam. "I am not going to chapel this morning. I must have that extra time for my biology. I can use it to good advantage, too. There won't be any noise or disturbance in the room," she added slyly.

Elfreda gave Miriam a reproachful glance over her shoulder as she left the dining room. "You'll be sorry for 'them cruel words' some day," she declared. "For instance, the next time my services as a chef are desired," and was gone.

Miriam left the dining room a little later, going directly upstairs. Grace and Anne lingered to talk with the girls still at breakfast, half expecting to hear the news of Ruth's father brought up. Nothing was said on the subject, however, and Grace wondered if Alberta Wicks and Mary Hampton could possibly have come to their senses and refused to take part in whatever mischief Kathleen had planned. How glad she would be, she reflected, if the two seniors, who had caused her so many unpleasant thoughts and moments turned out well after all.

After the service that morning she waited for Ruth, who was one of the last of the long procession of girls who filed out of the chapel. Arline was with her and made a rush for Grace the moment she caught sight of her. "I have been watching for you," she said eagerly.

"I haven't heard a word, and neither has Ruth. Perhaps they were more honorable than we believed them to be."

"I thought that, too," rejoined Grace. "It has been almost a week since I told Ruth. We may never hear a word concerning it."

"It wouldn't make much difference now," said Arline. "Ruth knows, and there isn't really anything to be said except that after many years' separation she may find her father. She need not care who knows that."

"It was the cruel shock to her that I thought of, and so did Kathleen West," explained Grace. "She seems determined to hurt some one's feelings by 'notoriety' methods. Her newspaper work has made her hard and unfeeling. She is always trying to dig up some one's private affairs and make them public property. I imagine our two seniors have placed a restraining hand on this last affair. I hope Mabel Ashe will never grow cruel and unfeeling—and dishonorable."

"She won't," predicted Arline. "Father knows many delightful newspaper women who are above reproach. Besides, Mabel will never remain on a newspaper long enough to change. There is a certain young lawyer in New York City who adores her, and I think she cares for him. There is no engagement yet, but there will be inside of a year or my name is not Arline Thayer."

"Really?" asked Grace, her eyes widening with interest. "She has never so much as intimated it to me."

"I know a little about it, for we have mutual friends in New York. Besides, Father knows the man. I've met him. He's a dear, and awfully handsome."

Having lingered to talk until the last moment the two girls were obliged to part abruptly and scurry off to their recitation rooms, which lay in different directions. They met late in the afternoon in the gymnasium to watch Elfreda's last practice playing before the game, but in their momentary basketball enthusiasm the topic of the morning's conversation was not touched upon.

The game between the sophomore and junior teams was looked upon as an event of extreme importance. Elfreda's love for the game and the story of her persistent effort to reduce her weight in order to glitter as a prominent basketball star had become familiar to not only her upper class friends, but throughout the college as well. She had several freshmen adorers, who sent her violets and vied with one another in entertaining her whenever she had an hour or two to spare them. In fact, J. Elfreda Briggs was becoming an important factor in the social life of Overton, with the satisfaction of knowing that she had won a place in the hearts of her admirers through her own merit.

Considerable preparation in the way of decorations had been made. About the balcony railing green and yellow bunting mingled with that of junior blue. The two front rows were well filled with members of the faculty, who wore ribbon rosettes with long ends and carried banners of blue, or green and yellow, as the case might be. The Semper Fidelis Club, resplendent in cocked hats of junior blue and wide blue crepe paper sashes fastened in the back with immense butterfly bows, occupied places directly behind the faculty. They had gone to the gymnasium an hour and a half before the game in order to secure these seats, and were now ranged in an eager, exultant row, impatiently awaiting the entrance of the two teams.

With the shrill notes of the whistle began one of the most stubborn conflicts ever waged between two Overton teams. From the instant the ball was put in play and the players leaped into action the interest of the spectators never wavered. During the first half of the game the sophomores valiantly contested every foot of the ground, and it was only at the very end of the half that the juniors succeeded in making the score six to four in their favor.

In the last half the doughty sophomores rose to the occasion and tied the score with their first play. Then Elfreda, with unerring aim, made a long overhand throw to basket that brought forth deafening applause from the spectators. The sophomores managed to gain two more points, but the juniors again managed not only to gain two points, but to pile up their score until a particularly brilliant play to basket on the part of Elfreda closed the last half with the glorious reckoning of seventeen to twelve in favor of the juniors.

Immediately a hubbub arose from the gallery. The Semper Fidelis Club burst forth into a victorious song they had been practising for the occasion, while another delegation of juniors also rent the air with their chant of triumph over their sophomore sisters.

After Elfreda had experienced the satisfaction of being escorted round the room by her classmates, who continued to sing spiritedly at least three different songs at the top of their lungs, she was hurried into the dressing room by the Semper Fidelis Club. The moment she was dressed she was seized by friendly hands and marched off to Vinton's to a dinner given by the club in honor of her. For the present, at least, she was the most important girl in college, and feeling the weight of her new-born fame, she was unusually silent, almost shy.

"Elfreda can't accustom herself to being a celebrity," laughed Miriam. "She is terribly embarrassed."

"That is really the truth," confessed Elfreda. "I've always wanted to be a basketball star, but it seems funny to have the girls make such a fuss over me."

"You deserve it!" exclaimed Gertrude Wells. "You were the pride of the team. I never want to see a better game. That last play of yours was a record breaker."

The other members of the club joined in Gertrude's praise of Elfreda's playing. The stout girl's face shone with happiness. To her it was one of the great moments of her college life.

It was after seven o'clock when the diners left Vinton's. The club gallantly escorted Elfreda to the very door of Wayne Hall and left her after singing to her and giving three cheers. Grace, Anne, Miriam, Arline, Ruth, Mildred Taylor and Laura Atkins were her body guard up the stairs. At the landing Laura Atkins called a halt and invited every one present to a jollification in her room that night in honor of Elfreda.

While Elfreda was explaining that she didn't wish the girls to go to any trouble for her, although her eyes shone with delight at being thus honored, the door bell rang repeatedly, and the maid, grumbling under her breath, admitted Emma Dean, who skipped up the stairs two at a time.

"I'm always late," she announced cheerfully, "but hardly ever too late. I stopped at the big bulletin board. I noticed a letter there addressed to you, Grace. It was marked 'Important' in one corner. I had half a mind to bring it with me, then—well—you know how one feels about meddling with some one else's mail."

"I'm sorry you didn't bring it with you. Don't hesitate to do so next time," returned Grace regretfully. "However, it won't take long to run across the campus for it. I'll go now before I take off my hat and coat. Thank you for telling me about it, Emma."

"You are welcome," called Emma after her as Grace ran to her room for her wraps. Always on the alert for home letters, under no circumstances could she have been content to wait quietly until the next day for the coveted mail. If it were from her mother or father she could read it over and over before bedtime and go to sleep happy in the possession of it, and if it were from one of her numerous friends it would be joyfully received.

The handwriting on the envelope Grace took from the bulletin board looked strangely familiar. Tearing it open, she glanced hastily over the few lines of the letter, an expression of incredulity in her eyes, for the note said:—

"MY DEAR MISS HARLOWE:—

"May I come to Wayne Hall to see you to-morrow evening at half-past seven o'clock? Please leave note in the bulletin board stating whether this will be convenient for you.

"Yours sincerely,
"ALBERTA WICKS."

Grace read the note again, then mechanically folding it, returned it to its envelope, and walked slowly back to Wayne Hall divided between her disappointment in the letter, and speculation as to the purport of Alberta Wicks's proposed call.

CHAPTER XXI

ALBERTA KEEPS HER PROMISE

During the following day Grace pondered not a little over the possible meaning of Alberta Wicks's note. She wrote an equally brief reply, stating that she would be at Wayne Hall the following night at the appointed time, and tried, unsuccessfully, to dismiss the matter from her mind. It persisted in recurring to her at intervals, and when, at exactly half-past seven o'clock, Alberta Wicks was ushered into the living room, Grace's heart beat a trifle faster as she went forward to greet her guest, who looked less haughty than usual, and who actually smiled faintly as she returned Grace's greeting.

"I know I am the last person you ever expected to see," began Alberta, looking embarrassed, "but I simply felt as though I must come here to-night. Are we likely to be interrupted?" she asked suddenly.

"Perhaps we had better go upstairs to my room," suggested Grace. "My roommate is away this evening."

"Thank you," replied the other girl. She followed Grace upstairs with an unaccustomed meekness that made Grace marvel as to what had suddenly wrought so marked a change in this hitherto disagreeable senior.

Once the two girls were seated opposite each other, Alberta leaned forward and said earnestly: "I know that you must dislike me very, very much, Miss Harlowe, and I always supposed that I disliked you even more, but I have lately come to the conclusion that I admire you more than any girl I know."

Grace looked at her guest in uncomprehending wonder. Could this be the sneering, insolent Miss Wicks who was speaking? There was no sign of a sneer on her face now. She spoke with a simple directness that could not fail to impress the most sceptical. "I have been hearing about you from a source entirely outside Overton," she continued, "from a Smith College senior who lives in Oakdale. She visited a friend of mine during the holidays. I live in Boston, you know."

"I didn't know," began Grace, then with a little exclamation: "It can't be possible! You don't mean Julia Crosby?"

"Yes," nodded Alberta. "I do mean Julia Crosby. Thanks to her, I have had my eyes opened to a good many things. I—am—sorry—for everything, Miss Harlowe." Her voice faltered. "I—never—saw—myself as I was—until Miss Crosby made me see. Directly after meeting her she asked me if I knew you, and I spoke slightingly of you. She said very decidedly that you were one of her dearest friends, and defended you to the skies. She told me about your saving her from drowning, and of how badly she had once behaved toward you, and how brave and loyal you were. Then we had a long talk and she made me promise to square things with you the minute I came back, but I haven't had the courage until to-day." She paused and looked appealingly at Grace.

Without hesitation Grace held out her hand. "I am not a very formidable person," she smiled. "I am so glad you know Julia Crosby, too. She must have told you of the good times we used to have together in Oakdale."

Alberta nodded. She could not yet trust her voice.

"Julia wanted me to go to Smith with her," Grace went on rapidly in order to give her guest a chance to recover herself. "At first I thought seriously of it, but later Anne and Miriam and I decided on Overton. And we haven't been disappointed, not for an hour! I wouldn't exchange Overton for any other college in the United States," she ended with loyal pride. "Don't you love Overton, Miss Wicks?"

"No," returned the other girl shortly. "It is too late for that sort of thing for me. I forfeited my right long ago. No one will miss me when I leave. Other than Mary, I have no real friends, even in my own class, and you know what most of the juniors think of us." Alberta's tone was very bitter. "Of course, we have no one but ourselves to blame, but just lately I've begun to wish that I had been different."

There was an awkward silence. Grace made a vain effort to think of something to say to this hitherto unapproachable senior who had suddenly become so humble. Before she could frame a reply Alberta continued almost sullenly:

"I don't know why I should care so much. But after Julia Crosby told me how you saved her life when she broke through the ice into the river and what a splendid girl you were, I felt awfully ashamed of myself. She talked to me and made me promise I would come to see you as soon as I returned to Overton. I am afraid I would have stayed away, though, if it hadn't been for something else."

Grace's eyes were frankly questioning, but she still said nothing.

"It is about that Miss West," said the senior, as though in answer to Grace's mute inquiry. "I am sorry to say that I encouraged her to do all sorts of revolutionary things when she first came here. I discovered she disliked you and your friends, and I was glad of it. I never lost an opportunity to fan the flame."

"But why did she dislike us?" asked Grace. "That is the thing none of us understand. We were prepared to like her because Mabel Ashe had written me, asking me to look out for her. You know they worked on the same newspaper. We did everything we could to make her feel at home, until suddenly she began to cut our acquaintance. Later on something happened that made her angry with me, but to this day none of us knows why she cut us in the first place."

"She never said a word to Mary or me about Mabel Ashe," declared Alberta in frowning surprise. "We supposed she had come to Wayne Hall as a stranger and had been snubbed by your crowd of girls. She was furiously angry with you because she wasn't asked to help with the bazaar. She wanted to be in the circus, and said you asked other freshmen and slighted her."

"And I never dreamed she would care," returned Grace wonderingly. "If we had only asked her to take part, all these unpleasantnesses might have been avoided. You see, we didn't intend to ask any freshmen, but we finally asked Myra Stone because she made such a darling doll. Oh, I'm so sorry."

"I wouldn't be if I were you," declared Alberta dryly. "Judging from what I know of her, I don't think she deserves much sympathy. I just prevented her from publishing Miss Denton's private affairs broadcast through the medium of her paper."

"You don't mean she—" began Grace.

Alberta nodded. "Yes, she wrote a story in a highly sensational style and brought it to me to read. She was going to send it to her paper, then mail copies of the edition in which the story appeared to a number of girls here. She had a long list, which she showed me, and wanted me to promise to help her address the papers and send them to the various girls. But after I had that talk with Julia Crosby I vowed within myself that the little time I had left at Overton should be devoted to some better cause than planning petty, silly ways of 'getting even.' I can't tell you how thankful I am that I have had this chance to live up to a little of what I promised myself I would do. There is just one thing I'd like to know, and that is the truth of the story concerning Miss Denton's father."

"I shall be glad to tell you all I know, which is really very little," answered Grace, and once more repeated the story of what their holiday visit to the old hunter had brought forth. "I wrote to Mr. Denton to the address in Nome the very next day after we were out at Jean's and have written once since then, and so has Ruth, but we have never received an answer. Still, I believe that we shall yet hear from him. I feel certain that he is still living. I really hated to tell Ruth, and raise her hopes only to destroy them again by having to say that he had never answered our letters, but we decided that it was best for her to know. She has been so brave and dear. We told Miss Thayer, and my three friends know it, too, but we don't want any one else to know unless Ruth really finds her father. It is her own personal affair, you see."

"But how did Miss West find it out?" was Alberta's question.

Grace shook her head. "Don't ask me," she said, a hint of scorn in her eyes. "I am so glad you prevailed upon her to give up the plan, for Ruth's sake and for her own as well."

"She was very determined at first, but she finally weakened and promised to drop the whole idea after she found that we were opposed to her plan," rejoined Alberta.

"You did a good day's work for Ruth," smiled Grace, holding out her hand to the other girl.

Alberta leaned forward in her chair and took Grace's hand in both of hers. "I wish I hadn't been so blind, Miss Harlowe. If I had only tried to know you long ago. There is so little of my college life left I can't hope to win your respect and liking."

"Don't try," laughed Grace. "You have my respect already, as for my liking, I'd be very glad to say 'Alberta Wicks is my friend.'"

"Can you say that and really mean it?" asked Alberta almost incredulously.

"I would not say it unless I were quite certain that I meant it," Grace assured her. "Your coming here to-night proved clearly that you were ready to forget all past differences. Then, why should I hold spite or nurse a grievance? Now, we are not going to say another word about it. I should like to have you spend the evening with me. I am going to invite Miriam and Elfreda to a conversation and tea party in honor of you."

"Oh, no!" protested Alberta, half rising. "They wouldn't come. Elfreda will never forgive me for causing her so much trouble."

"Elfreda has forgotten all about what happened to her as a freshman. At least she has forgiven you," added Grace. "She and Miriam will be glad to know that we are friends." Grace spoke confidently, though she did have a brief instant of doubt as to just how Elfreda would regard Alberta's belated repentance. To her intense relief, however, when leaving Alberta for a moment she ran down the hall to invite Miriam and Elfreda, the one-time stout girl offered no other comment than a grumbled, "Just like you, Grace Harlowe."

"But will you come to my tea party?" persisted Grace.

"Of course we will," accepted Miriam.

"She knows about it all, she knows, she knows," droned Elfreda. "What's the use in asking me anything when Miriam is here?"

"All right." Grace turned to go. "I'll expect to see both of you within the next ten minutes. Don't change your mind after I have gone."

"See here, Grace Harlowe!" Elfreda rose from her chair and walked toward Grace. "I should like to know—"

"Don't say it, Elfreda," interrupted Grace. "Just say you'll come. If you don't come Alberta will go back to Stuart Hall, disappointed and resentful at having her friendly overtures rejected. She is at the critical stage now, Elfreda, dear, and needs encouragement and cheering up. She is a trifle bitter, and has the blues, too, although she is too stiff-necked to admit it."

"You needn't be afraid. I wasn't going to throw cold water on the tea party. Of course we'll attend, and bring the whole two pounds of fruit cake we bought to-day with us. You can take our new cups and saucers, too, can't she, Miriam? What I should like to know is how it all happened."

"I can't stop to tell you now. Wait until Anne comes home to-night and we'll congregate. I want to see Arline, too. I have a plan that just came to me a little while ago, and I should like to hear what you think of it. I must hurry back to my guest. Come to my room as soon as you can."

"Now I wonder what she has on her mind?" smiled Miriam. "I imagine it has something to do with Alberta Wicks."

"Do you know," remarked Elfreda, looking up with a sudden tender light in her usually matter-of-fact face, "there's a line in 'Hamlet' that always makes me think of Grace. It's the one in which Hamlet speaks of his father. He says, 'I shall never look upon his like again.' Substituting 'her' for 'his,' that is exactly what I think about Grace."

The next morning Grace awoke with the feeling of one who has had something disagreeable suddenly disappear from her life. "What happened last night?" she asked herself, then smiled as the memory of what had passed the evening before returned. "I'm so glad," she said half under her breath.

"Glad of what?" asked Anne, who, wrapped in her kimono, sat sleepily on the edge of her bed, trying to make up her mind to stay awake.

"That Alberta Wicks came to see me," replied Grace. "I hate quarrels and misunderstandings, Anne, yet I seem destined to become involved in them. Do you suppose it is because I have a quarrelsome disposition?" Grace had slipped out of bed, and, wrapping herself in her bath robe, trotted across the room and seated herself beside Anne, one arm thrown across her friend's shoulder.

"Quarrelsome? You are a positive snapping turtle," Anne assured her gravely. "I am so glad I have only one more year of your detestable society before me. Now you know the truth. Kill me if you must," she added in melodramatic tones.

"I'll be merciful and let you live until after Easter," laughed Grace. "That reminds me, Anne. I am going to ask Ruth to go home with us. I know she is anxious to talk with Jean, although she wouldn't say so for the world. She is always in mortal fear of intruding. Arline knows that I am going to invite Ruth. I'm going there this very morning if I can manage to hustle down to her room before my biology hour," concluded Grace, rising from the couch with an energy that nearly precipitated Anne to the floor. "We forgot to congregate last night after Alberta went home, it was so late. I'll tell you my plan to-night. But we won't try to carry it out until after Easter."

Ruth cried a little on Grace's comforting shoulder when, an hour later, she delivered her Easter invitation. To Grace's satisfaction, she accepted without a protesting word. She remembered only that Jean, the hunter, had known her father and she had a wistful desire to take old Jean by the hand for her father's sake. Arline had promised to spend Easter with Grace, but her father had planned a trip to the

Bermudas for her and Ruth. Realizing that it would be best for Ruth to go to Oakdale, she cheerfully put aside her own personal desire for Ruth's companionship and urged Ruth to go home with Grace.

Elfreda had accepted Laura Atkins's invitation to spend Easter with her, and was already convulsing the three Oakdale girls with excerpts from conversations to take place, supposedly, between herself and Laura's learned father. "I have been reading up a lot on the pterodactyl and ichthyosaurus and other small, playful animals of the beginning of the world variety," she confided to Miriam. "I expect to astonish him."

"I am reasonably sure that you will," was Miriam's mirthful reply. "I wish you were coming home with me, instead."

"So do I." Elfreda's shrewd eyes grew wistful. "I know I'd have the best time ever if I went home with you, but I feel as though I ought to go with Laura. She would have been so disappointed if I had refused her invitation. That sounds conceited, doesn't it? But you can see how things are, can't you?"

"I can, indeed," returned Miriam, and the significance of her tone left no doubt in Elfreda's mind regarding her roommate's understanding of things.

CHAPTER XXII

GRACE'S PLAN

The Easter vacation slipped away at the same appalling rate of speed that had marked the passing of all Grace's holidays at home. There were so many pleasant things to do and so many old friends to welcome her return to Oakdale that she sighed regretfully to think she could not possibly accept one half of the invitations that poured in upon her from all sides.

Nora and Jessica had come from the conservatory to spend Easter at home, so had the masculine half of the "Eight Originals Plus Two." Then, too, the Phi Sigma Tau, with the exception of Eleanor Savelli, had renewed their vows of unswerving loyalty, and their numerous sessions ate up the time. There was one day set aside, however, on which the little clan had paid a visit to Jean, the old hunter, and Ruth had experienced the satisfaction of seeing and talking with a man who had been her father's friend. The old woodsman had been equally delighted to take Arthur Denton's child by the hand, and the tears had run down his brown, weather-beaten cheeks as he looked into Ruth's face and exclaimed at the resemblance to her father that he saw there. "You shall yet hear. You shall yet see, Mamselle," he had prophesied with a fullness of belief that made Grace resolve to keep on writing to the address Jean had given her for a year at least, whether or not she received a line in return. She, too, felt confident that Arthur Denton still lived.

She was, therefore, more disappointed than she cared to admit when, on returning to Overton, she failed to find an answer to the letters which she had sent to Nome at stated intervals. Ruth, apprehensive and sick at heart, by reason of hope deferred, was striving to be brave in spite of the bitterness of her disappointment. From the beginning she had sternly determined not to be buoyed by false hopes, then if she never heard from the letters that she and Grace had sent speeding northward, she would have nothing to disturb her peace of mind other than the regret that her dream had never come true. Yet it was hard not to think of her father and not to hope.

A late Easter made a short April, and May was well upon them before the students of Overton College awoke to the realization that it was only a matter of days until the senior class would be graduated and gone; that the juniors would be seniors, the sophomores juniors, and even the humblest freshman would taste the sweetness of sophomoreship.

To Grace the rapid passing of the last days of her junior year brought a certain indefinable sadness. There were times when she wished herself a freshman, that she were ending her first year of college life rather than the third. Only one more year and it would all be over. Then what lay beyond? Grace never went further than that. She had no idea as to what life would mean to her when her college days were past. She had not yet found her work. Anne would, no doubt, return to her profession. Miriam intended to study music in Leipsig at the same conservatory where Eleanor Savelli's father and mother had met. Elfreda had long since announced her intention of becoming a lawyer. Ruth fully expected to teach, and even dainty Arline had hinted that she might take up settlement work.

Grace was thinking rather soberly of all this, late on Saturday afternoon as she walked slowly across the campus toward Wayne Hall. "I really ought to begin to think seriously of my future work," she thought. "Father and Mother would only be too glad to have me stay at home with them, but I feel as though I ought to 'be up and doing with a heart for any fate' instead of just being a home girl. Miss Duncan said the last time I talked with her that I would some day hit upon my work when I least expected it. I hope it will happen soon. Oh, there goes Alberta Wicks!" she cried aloud. "I must see her at once. Alberta!"

Alberta Wicks, who was within hailing distance, turned abruptly and walked toward Grace.

"Where have you been of late? I haven't seen you. Did you receive my note?" asked Grace, holding out her hand to the other girl.

"Yes," returned Alberta, a slow red creeping into her cheeks. "I meant to come to Wayne Hall, but——" She paused, then said with a touch of her old defiance, "I might as well tell you the truth, I am rather afraid of the girls there."

"'Afraid of the girls!'" repeated Grace. "Why are you afraid of them, Alberta?"

"Because I've been so disagreeable," was the low reply. "They were very sweet with me the night of your tea party, but I felt as though they bore with me for your sake."

"On the contrary, they were pleased to entertain you," replied Grace with a sincerity that even Alberta could not doubt. "I hope you will come again soon, and I wish you would bring Miss Hampton with you."

"Thank you," returned Alberta, but her hesitating reply was equivalent to refusal.

"She wants to come, but she still believes we don't like her," reflected Grace, as Alberta said good-bye and walked away with an almost dejected expression on her face. "Now is the time to put my plan into execution. I had forgotten it until seeing Alberta brought it back to me. I must propose it to the girls to-night."

From the evening on which Alberta had kept her promise to Julia Crosby and come to Wayne Hall to make peace, Grace had experienced a strong desire to help her sweeten and brighten the last days of her college life. With this thought in mind she had evolved the idea of giving Alberta and Mary a surprise party at Wellington House and inviting the Semper Fidelis girls as well as certain popular seniors and juniors who would be sure to add to the gayety of the affair. But when after dinner she broached the subject to her three friends, who had seated themselves in an expectant row on her couch to hear her plan, she was wholly unprepared for the amount of opposition with which it was received.

"I can't see why we should exert ourselves to make things pleasant for those two girls," grumbled Elfreda. "For almost three years they have taken particular pains to make matters unpleasant for us. The other night I treated Miss Wicks civilly for your sake, Grace, not because I am fond of her."

"I am afraid you will have considerable trouble in making the other girls promise to help you," demurred Miriam. "Neither Miss Wicks nor Miss Hampton have ever done anything to endear themselves to the girls here at Overton. Personally, I believe in letting well-enough alone in this case. If you wish to entertain them at Wayne Hall, of course we will stand by you. But I don't believe it would be wise to attempt to give a semi-public demonstration. It would be very humiliating for you if the girls refused to help you."

"But if they promise to help they are not likely to break their word," argued Grace, "and I shall make a personal call upon every girl on my list."

"Aren't you afraid that a 'list' may cause jealousy and ill-feeling on the part of certain girls who are not included in it?" was Anne's apprehensive question.

"And you, too, Anne!" exclaimed Grace in a hurt voice, looking her reproach. "No, I don't see why it should cause any ill-feeling whatever. We are not making it a class affair. There will be perhaps thirty girls invited. Aside from the surety that we'll have a good time, I believe we will be going far toward displaying the true Overton spirit. Of course, if you girls feel that you don't wish to enter into this with me, then I shall have to go on alone, for I am determined to do it. At least you can't gracefully refuse to come to the surprise party," she ended, with a little catch in her voice.

"Grace Harlowe, you big goose!" exclaimed Elfreda, springing to Grace's side and winding both arms about her. "Did you believe for one instant that we wouldn't stand by you no matter what you planned to do? I am ashamed of myself. If it hadn't been for me, you would never have had any trouble with either Alberta Wicks or Mary Hampton. Plan whatever you like, and I set my hand and seal upon it that I'll aid you and abet you to the fullest extent of my powers."

"And so will I," cried Miriam. "I am sorry I croaked."

"And to think I was a wet blanket, too," murmured Anne, patting one of Grace's hands.

"You are perfect angels, all of you," declared Grace, her gray eyes shining. "I know I am always dragging you into things, and making you help me for friendship's sake."

"But they are always the right sort of things," retorted Elfreda, with an affectionate loyalty.

"Let us atone for our defection by making ourselves useful," proposed Anne, picking up paper and pencil from the writing table. "I'll write the names of those eligible to the surprise party if you'll supply them."

After considerable discussion, erasing, crossing out and re-establishing the list of names was finally declared to be satisfactory.

"Is there any particular friend of either of these girls that we have forgotten to include?" asked Anne, as she carefully scanned the list.

"What of Kathleen West?" asked Elfreda.

Grace shook her head. "I believe it would be better not to ask her," she said. "She wouldn't come; besides, she might—" Grace stopped. She had been tempted to say that Kathleen would be likely to tell tales and spoil the surprise.

"I know what you were going to say. You believe she would tell Alberta our plans and spoil the party," was Elfreda's blunt comment. "Well, so do I believe it. Any one can see that."

Grace smiled at Elfreda's emphatic statement.

"It is wiser not to ask her," she said again. "There are four of us, and we can count on Arline and Ruth; that leaves twenty-four girls to be invited. Divided, that is six girls to each one of us. You must each choose the six girls you will agree to see and make it your business to invite them to the party. Try to make them promise to come, for we don't want to change the list."

"What are we going to have to eat?" asked Elfreda. "That is an extremely important feature of any jollification. I always think of things to eat, even though I don't eat them. Just thinking of them can't make one stout, and it is a world of satisfaction."

"We had better have different kinds of sandwiches, olives and pickles, and what else?" asked Grace.

"Ice cream and cake. We might have salted nuts and lemonade, too," added Miriam.

"It sounds good to me," averred Elfreda, relapsing into slang. "But don't rely on the girls to bring this stuff. Assess them fifty cents apiece with the understanding that another tax will be levied if necessary."

"That is sound advice," laughed Miriam, "but it means that the duty of making of the sandwiches must fall upon us."

"I guess I can stand it," nodded Elfreda with a sudden generosity. "I'll take the sandwich making upon myself, if you say so. You all know perfectly well that I can neither be equalled nor surpassed when it comes to the 'eats' problem. Candidly, I'm ashamed of myself because I didn't respond when Grace first asked me to help, and this sandwich task is going to be my act of atonement. So, Anne, you and Miriam had better get busy, too, and decide what yours will be, for we've all been found guilty of lacking college spirit, and we've got to make good."

"I will pledge myself to collect the money for the refreshments as a further act of atonement," volunteered Anne.

"And I will do the shopping for you when the money is collected," promised Miriam. "Thanks to the careful training of J. Elfreda Briggs, I know what to buy and where to buy it."

"But you are leaving nothing for me to do," protested Grace.

"There will be plenty of things for you to do," declared Elfreda. "You will have to keep an eye on us and see that we perform our tasks with diplomacy and skill."

"It requires a great deal of diplomacy to make sandwiches, doesn't it, Elfreda?" was Anne's innocent observation.

"You know very well I wasn't referring to the making of the sandwiches," retorted Elfreda, with a good-natured grin. "It is the delivering of the invitations that is going to require a wily, sugar-coated tongue. The majority of the girls are not fond of either Alberta Wicks or Mary Hampton. The very ones you believe will help you may prove to be the most prejudiced."

"I am well aware of that fact," flung back Grace laughingly. "I received an unexpected demonstration of it a few moments ago."

"So you did," responded Elfreda unabashed. "I hadn't forgotten it, either. Therefore I repeat that you will have your hands full managing the ethical side of this surprise party. You will have to interview the girls we can't persuade to come, for there are sure to be some of them who will raise the same objections that we did, and if they do accept, it will be only to please Grace Harlowe."

CHAPTER XXIII

WHAT EMMA DEAN FORGOT

The surprise party did much toward placing Alberta Wicks and Mary Hampton on a friendly footing with the members of their own class and the juniors. Strange to relate, there had been little or no reluctance exhibited by those invited in accepting their invitations, and as a final satisfaction to Grace the night of the party was warm and moonlit.

The astonishment of the two seniors can be better imagined than described. Grace had purposely made an engagement to spend the evening with them, and under pretense of having Alberta Wicks try over a new song, had inveigled them to the living room, where the company of girls had trooped in upon them, and a merry evening had ensued.

Wholly unused to friendly attentions from their classmates, Alberta and Mary, formerly self-assured even to arrogance, did the honors of the occasion with a touch of diffidence that went far toward establishing them on an entirely new basis at Overton, and they said good-night to their guests with a delightful feeling of comradeship that had never before been theirs.

It had been agreed upon by the Semper Fidelis girls that they should extend the right hand of fellowship as often as possible to the two seniors during the short time left them at Overton. It was Grace who had proposed this. "We must do all we can to help them fill the last of their college days with good times. Then they can never forget what a great honor it is to call Overton 'Alma Mater,'" she had argued with an earnestness that could not be gainsaid.

Now that this particular shadow had lifted, Grace was still concerned over her utter failure to keep her word to Mabel Ashe regarding the newspaper girl. When Kathleen had discovered that Alberta Wicks and Mary Hampton now numbered themselves among Grace's friends, she religiously avoided the two seniors as well as the Semper Fidelis girls. She became sullen and moody, apparently lost all interest in breaking rules and studied with an earnestness that evoked the commendation of the faculty, and caused her to be classed with the "digs" by the more frivolous-minded freshmen. Her reputation for dashing off clever bits of verse also became established, and her themes were frequently read in the freshman English classes and occasionally in sophomore English, too. In spite of her literary achievements, however, she remained as unpopular as ever. To the girls who knew her she was too changeable to be relied upon, and her sarcastic manner discouraged those who ventured to be friendly.

"If I haven't been able to keep my word to Mabel it isn't because I have not tried," Grace Harlowe murmured half aloud, as she walked toward her favorite seat under a giant elm at the lower end of the campus, an unopened letter in her hand. Grace tore open the envelope and immediately became absorbed in the contents of the letter. "I wish she could come up here for commencement," she sighed, "and I wish she knew the truth about Kathleen West. I can't write it. It would seem so unfair and contemptible to present my side of the story to Mabel without giving Kathleen a chance to present hers. That is, if she really considers that she has one."

"I knew I'd find you here," called a disconsolate voice, and Emma Dean appeared from behind a huge flowering bush. "I've a terrible confession to make, and there's no time like the present for admitting my sins of omission and commission. Please put a decided accent on omission."

"Now what have you forgotten to do?" laughed Grace. "It can't be anything very serious."

"You won't laugh when I tell you," returned Emma, looking sober. "I shall never be agreeable and promise to deliver a message or anything else for any one again. I am not to be trusted. Here is the cause of all my sorrow." She handed Grace a large, square envelope with the contrite explanation: "Words can't tell you how sorry I am. It has been in the pocket of my heavy coat since the week before I went home for the Easter holidays. I went over to the big bulletin board the day before you went home and saw this letter addressed to you. I wish I had left it there, as I did last time. There was one for me, too, so I put them both in my coat pocket, intending to give you yours the moment I reached Wayne Hall. But before I was half way across the campus I met the Emerson twins, and they literally dragged me into Vinton's for a sundae. By the time I reached the hall, all remembrance of the letters had passed from my mind.

"I didn't take my heavy coat home with me, and when I came back to Overton the weather had grown warm, so I did not wear it again. This afternoon it fell on the floor of my closet, and when I picked it up I noticed something white at the top of one of the pockets. There! Now I've confessed and I shall not blame you if you are cross with me. My letter didn't amount to much. It was from a cousin of mine, whose letters always bore me to desperation. Now, say all the mean things to me that you like. I'm resigned," invited Emma, closing her eyes and folding her hands across her breast.

"I'm not going to scold you, Emma," declared Grace, laughing a little. "I wonder who this can be from? The postmark is almost obliterated. However, I'll soon see."

"Do you want me to go on about my business?" was Emma's pointed question.

"Certainly not. Pardon me while I read this. Then I'll walk to the Hall with you. It is almost dinner time." As Grace unfolded the letter the inside sheet fell from it to the ground. As she bent to pick it up her eyes lingered upon the signature with an expression of unbelieving amazement stamped upon her face. Then she glanced down the first page of the letter.

"Oh, it can't be true! It's too wonderful!" she gasped. "Oh, Emma, Emma, if I had only received this the day it came!"

"I knew it was something important," groaned Emma. "And I was trying to be so helpful."

Unmindful of Emma's remorseful utterance, Grace went on excitedly: "Only think, Emma, it is from Ruth's father. He is alive and well and frantic with joy over the news that Ruth did not die in that terrible wreck." Grace sprang from her seat and seized Emma by the arm. "Come on," she urged, "I must tell the girls at once."

Grace ran all the way to Wayne Hall, and bursting into her room pounced upon Anne and hustled her unceremoniously into Miriam's room, where Elfreda and Miriam viewed their noisy entrance with tolerant eyes. A moment afterward Emma Dean appeared, out of breath. In a series of excited sentences, Grace told the glorious news. "But I must read you what he says," she said, her eyes very bright.

"MY DEAR MISS HARLOWE:—

"What can I say to you who have sent me the most welcome message I ever received? It is as though the dead had come to life. To think that my baby daughter, my little Ruth, still lives, and has fought her way to friends and education. It is almost beyond belief. I cannot fittingly express by letter the feeling of gratitude which overwhelms me when I think of your generous and whole-souled interest in me and my child. I have certain matters here in Nome to which I must attend, then I shall start for the States, and once there proceed east with all speed. It will not be advisable for you to answer this letter, as I shall have started on my journey before your answer could possibly reach me. I shall telegraph Ruth as soon as I arrive in San Francisco. I have not written her as yet, because you said in your letter to me that you did not wish her to know until you had heard from me. I thank you for trying to shield her from needless pain, and I am longing for the day when I can look into Ruth's eyes and call her daughter. Believe me, my appreciation of your kindness to me and to Ruth lies too deep for words. With the hope that I shall be in Overton before many weeks to claim my own, and thank you and your friends personally,

"Yours in deep sincerity,
"ARTHUR NORTHRUP DENTON."

"Well, if that isn't in the line of a sensation, then my name isn't Josephine Elfreda Briggs! And to think Ruth's father has actually materialized and is coming to Overton? When did you receive the letter, Grace?"

"It came just before the Easter vacation," interposed Emma Dean bravely, without giving Grace a chance to answer. "I might as well tell you. I took it from the big bulletin board, put it in my coat pocket to bring to Grace and forgot it. Don't all speak at once." Emma bowed her head, her hands over her ears.

Then an immediate buzz of conversation arose, and Emma came in for a deserved amount of good-natured teasing.

"What is the date of the letter!" asked Elfreda.

"The twenty-sixth of February," replied Grace. "It must have been on the way for weeks."

"And in Emma's pocket longer," was Miriam's sly comment.

"But he should have arrived long before this," persisted Elfreda. "I wonder if he received Ruth's letter."

"Perhaps he didn't start as soon as he intended," said Anne.

"That may be so. Nevertheless, he has had plenty of time to attend to his affairs and come here, too," declared Elfreda. "I wouldn't be surprised to see him almost any day."

"Wouldn't it be splendid if he were to come here in time to see Ruth usher at commencement?" smiled Grace.

"He'd better hurry, then," broke in Emma Dean, "for commencement is only two weeks off. Shall you tell Ruth? Who is going with you to tell her, and when are you going?"

"After dinner, all of us," announced Elfreda. "Aren't we, Grace?"

Grace nodded.

"Then I shall join the band," announced Emma. "Although I proved a delinquent and untrustworthy messenger, still you must admit that at last I delivered my message."

CHAPTER XXIV

CONCLUSION

The last of June, in addition to its reputed wealth of roses, brought with it exceedingly hot weather, but to the members of the senior and junior classes, whose eyes were fixed upon commencement, the warm weather was a matter of minor importance. It was the first Overton commencement in which the three Oakdale girls had taken part, and greatly to their satisfaction they had been detailed to usher at the commencement exercises. Arline, Ruth, Gertrude Wells, the Emersons and Emma Dean had also acted as ushers, and on the evening of commencement day the Emerson twins had given a porch party to the other "slaves of the realm," as they had laughingly styled themselves.

It had been a momentous week, and the morning after commencement day Grace awoke with the disturbing thought that her trunk remained still unpacked, that she had two errands to do, and that she had promised to meet Arline Thayer at Vinton's at half-past nine o'clock that morning.

"I am glad it isn't eight o'clock yet," she commented to Anne, as she stood before the mirror looking very trim and dainty in her tailored suit of dark blue. "I'm going to put on my hat now, then I won't have to come upstairs again. I'll do my errands first, then it will be time to meet Arline, and I'll be here in time for luncheon. After that I must pack my trunk, and if I hurry I shall still have some time to spare. Our train doesn't leave until four o'clock. Will you telephone for the expressman, Anne?"

Anne, who was busily engaged in trying to make room in the tray of her trunk for a burned wood handkerchief box which she had overlooked, looked up long enough to acquiesce. "There!" she exclaimed as the box finally slipped into place, "that is something accomplished. Hereafter, I shall leave this box at home. Every time I pack my trunk I am sure to find it staring me in the face from some corner of the room when I haven't a square inch of space left. I'll keep my handkerchiefs in the top drawer of the chiffonier next year."

"I wish I had no packing to do," sighed Grace. "You never seem to mind it."

"That is because I am a trouper, and troupers live in their trunks," smiled Anne. "Packing and unpacking never dismay me."

"Isn't it fortunate, Anne, that our commencement happened a week before that of the boys? We can be at home for a day or two before we go to M—— to attend their commencement."

"I can't realize that our boys are men, and about to go out into the world, each one to his own work," said Anne. "They will always seem just boys to us, won't they?"

"Yes, the spirit of youth will remain with them as long as they live," prophesied Grace wisely, "because they will always be interested in things. And if one lives every day for all it is worth and goes on to the next day prepared to make the best of whatever it may bring forth, one can never grow old in spirit. Look at Mrs. Gray. She never will be 'years old,' she will always be 'years young.' I am so anxious to see Father and Mother and Mrs. Gray and the girls, but I hate saying good-bye to Overton. Every year it seems to grow dearer."

"That is because it has been our second home," was Anne's soft rejoinder.

A knock at the door, followed by a peremptory summons in Elfreda's voice, "Come on down to breakfast," ended the little talk.

By half-past eight o'clock Grace was on her way toward Main Street, bent on disposing of her errands with all possible speed. The vision of her yawning trunk, flanked by piles of clothing waiting patiently to be put in it, loomed large before her. Later on, keeping her appointment with Arline, she heroically tore herself from that fascinating young woman's society and hurried toward Wayne Hall, filled with laudable intentions. Anne had finished her packing and departed to pay a farewell visit to Ruth Denton.

"Oh, dear," sighed Grace, "I hate to begin. I suppose I had better put these heavy things in first." She reached for her heavy blue coat and sweater, slowly depositing them in the bottom of the trunk. Her raincoat followed the sweater, and she was in the act of folding her blue serge dress, when a knock sounded on the door, and the maid proclaimed in a monotonous voice, "Telegram, Miss Harlowe."

The blue serge dress was thrown into the trunk, and Grace dashed from the room and down the stairs at the maid's heels. Her father and mother were Grace's first thought. What if something dreadful had happened to either of them! The bare idea of a telegram thrilled Grace with apprehension. Her fingers trembled as she signed the messenger's book and tore open the envelope. One glance at the telegram and with an inarticulate cry Grace darted up the stairs and down the hall to her room. Stopping only long enough to seize her hat, she made for the stairs, the telegram clutched tightly in her hand. "Oh, if Anne or Miriam were only here," she breathed, as she paused for an instant at Mrs. Elwood's gate to look up and down the street, then set off in the direction of the campus. At the edge of the campus she paused again, glancing anxiously about her in the vain hope of spying Ruth or Miriam, then she started across the campus toward Morton House. As she neared her destination, the front door of the hall opened and a familiar figure appeared. It was followed by another figure, and with a little exclamation of satisfaction Grace redoubled her pace. "Ruth! Arline!" she cried, her face alight: "Can't you guess? It has come at last. Here it is. Read it, Ruth."

Ruth had turned very pale, and was staring at Grace in mute, questioning fashion. "You don't mean — —" her voice died away in a startled gasp.

"I do, I do," caroled Grace, tears of sheer happiness rising in her gray eyes. "Read it, Ruth. Oh, I am so glad for your sake. Three more hours and you will see him. It seems like a fairytale."

Ruth stood still, reading the telegram over and over: "Arrive Overton 2:40. Will you and Ruth meet me? Arthur N. Denton."

"And to think," said Arline, in awe-stricken tones, "that Ruth is actually going to see her father!"

"My very own father." The tenderness in Ruth's voice brought the tears to Arline's blue eyes. Grace was making no effort to conceal the fact that her own were running over.

"You mustn't cry, girls," faltered Ruth. "It's the happiest day of—my—life." Then she buried her face in her hands and ran into the house. Grace and Arline followed, to find her huddled on the lowest step of the stairs, her slender shoulders shaking.

"I—I can't help it," she sobbed. "You would cry, too, if after being driven from pillar to post ever since you were little, you'd suddenly find that there was some one in the world who loved you and wanted to take care of you."

"Of course you can't help crying," soothed Grace, stroking the bowed head. "Arline and I cried, too. This is one of the great moments of your life."

"Dear little chum," said Arline softly, sitting down beside Ruth and putting her arms around the weeping girl, "your wish has been granted."

An eloquent silence fell upon the trio for a moment, which was broken by the sound of voices in the upstairs hall. Ruth and Arline rose simultaneously from the stairs. "Come up to my room," urged Arline, "and we will finish our cry in private."

"I have no more tears to shed," smiled Grace, "and I dare not go to your room."

"Dare not?" inquired Arline.

"I haven't finished my packing, and our train leaves at four-thirty. Oh!" Grace sprang to her feet in sudden alarm. "I asked Anne to telephone for the expressman. Perhaps he has called for my trunk, and gone by this time. If he has, I shall have to reopen negotiations with the express company at once in order that it shall reach the station in time. Will you meet me at the station at a quarter-past two o'clock, or can you stop for me at the Hall?"

"I'll be at the Hall at two o'clock," promised Ruth.

Filled with commendable determination to finish her packing as speedily as possible, Grace hurried home and up the stairs, unpinning her hat as she ran. Dashing into her room, she dropped her hat on her couch, then stared about her in amazement. The piles of clothing she had left had disappeared, and, yes, her trunk had also vanished. "Where—" she began, when the door opened and three figures precipitated themselves upon her.

"Don't say we never did anything for you," cried Elfreda.

"We didn't overlook a single thing," assured Anne.

"It isn't every one who can secure the services of professional trunk packers."

> "'Will you, won't you, will you, won't you,
> Come and join the dance?'"

caroled Elfreda off the key, as she did a true mock turtle shuffle around Grace. Joining hands, the three girls hemmed Grace in and pranced about her.

"What is going on in here?" demanded Emma Dean, appearing in the doorway. "Is the mere idea of being seniors going to your heads?"

"I ought to be the one to dance, Emma," laughed Grace. "I went out of here with my room in chaos and my trunk unpacked, and came back to find it not only packed but gone. Thank you, girls," she nodded affectionately to her chums.

"No one exhibited any such tender thoughtfulness for me," commented Emma. "I had to wrestle with my packing unaided and alone. And how things do pile up! I could hardly find a place for all my stuff."

"Oh, I almost forgot my great news," cried Grace. Then she produced the telegram, and a buzz of excited conversation began which lasted until the luncheon bell rang.

Ruth was punctual to the moment, and after receiving the affectionate congratulations of the girls, she and Grace started for the station on the, to Ruth, most eventful errand of her young life.

"How shall I know him, Grace, and how will he know me?" she said tremulously.

"I don't know," returned Grace rather blankly. "That part of it hadn't occurred to me. Still, Overton is only a small city, and there won't be many incoming passengers. It's a case of outgoing passengers this week. I have an idea that we shall know him," she concluded.

When, at exactly 2:40, the train pulled into the station, two pairs of eyes were fixed anxiously on the few travelers that left the train. Suddenly Grace's hand caught Ruth's arm, "There he is! Oh, Ruth, isn't he splendid? Come on. Don't be afraid. I feel certain he is Arthur Northrup Denton."

Seizing Ruth's hand, she led her, unresisting, to meet a tall, broad-shouldered, smooth-faced man, whose piercing gray eyes constantly scanned the various persons scattered along the platform. His brown hair was touched with gray at the temples, and his keen, resolute face bespoke unfaltering purpose and power.

With Grace to think was to act. She took an impulsive step toward the tall stranger, confronting him with, "I am Grace Harlowe. I am sure you are Mr. Denton."

"Yes, I am Arthur Denton, and ––"

"This is your daughter, Ruth," declared Grace hurriedly, pushing Ruth gently forward. An instant later the few persons lingering on the station platform saw the tall stranger fold the slender figure of Ruth in a long embrace.

"I was sure you were Ruth's father," declared Grace as, a little later, they were speeding through the streets of Overton in the taxicab Mr. Denton had engaged at the station. "The moment I saw you I felt that you could be no one else."

Ruth sat with her hand in her father's, an expression of ineffable tenderness on her small face. She was content to listen to him and Grace without joining in the conversation. Her greatest wish had been fulfilled and she was experiencing a joy too deep for words. Mr. Denton explained to them that his long silence had been due to a series of misadventures that had befallen him on his way from Alaska to San Francisco. He had received only one letter from Grace and none from Ruth, as he had left Nome directly after receiving Grace's letter. The others had evidently reached Nome after his departure and had not been forwarded to him. The boat on which he had taken passage had been wrecked and he had barely escaped drowning. He had been rescued by an Indian fisherman from the icy waters of Bering Sea, and taken to his hut, where for days he had lain ill from exposure to the elements.

At the earliest possible moment he had embarked for San Francisco, then journeyed east. He had purposely refrained from telegraphing until within a day's journey from Overton, fearing that something might occur to delay his meeting with his daughter.

Ruth, who had already planned to remain in Overton during the summer and work at dressmaking, smiled in rapture as she heard her father plan a long sight-seeing trip through the west which would last until time for her return to college in the fall. They drove with Grace to Wayne Hall, promising to return to the station in time to meet her friends and say good-bye to her, Mr. Denton assuring her that he hoped some day to repay the debt of gratitude which he owed her.

Three familiar figures ran downstairs to meet Grace as she stepped into the hall.

"We've been waiting patiently for you," announced Elfreda.

"Did he materialize?" from Anne.

"What do you think of him?" was Miriam's quick question.

"Come into the living-room and I'll tell you," said Grace. "We won't have much time to talk, though. It is after three o'clock now."

"No; come upstairs to our room," invited Elfreda. "We have a special reason for asking you."

Grace obediently accompanied the three girls upstairs. The first thing that attracted her eye was a tray containing a tall pitcher of fruit lemonade and four glasses. Elfreda stepped to the table and began pouring the lemonade. When she had filled the glasses she handed them, in turn, to each girl. "To our senior year," she said solemnly, raising her glass. "May it be the best of all. Drink her down."

"What a nice idea," smiled Grace as she set down her glass.

"It was Elfreda's proposal," said Miriam. "She made the lemonade, too."

"Then let us drink to her." Grace reached for her glass and Miriam for the pitcher.

"I'll do the honors this time," declared Miriam. "Here's to the Honorable Josephine Elfreda Briggs, expert brewer of lemonade, model roommate and loyal friend."

"Oh, now," protested Elfreda, "what made you spoil everything? I was just beginning to enjoy myself."

"The pleasure is all ours," retorted Anne.

"Besides, you are getting nothing but your just deserts. We are only glad to have a chance to demonstrate our deep appreciation of your many lovely qualities, Miss Briggs," she ended mischievously.

"Yes, Miss Briggs," laughed Grace, "you are indispensable to this happy band, Miss Briggs. You must be blind if you can't see that."

"Very blind indeed, Miss Briggs," agreed Miriam Nesbit. "But because you are so blind, Miss Briggs, I shall endeavor, in a few well chosen words, Miss Briggs, to make you see what is so plain to the rest of us." Whereupon Miriam launched forth into a funny little eulogy of Elfreda and her good works which caused the stout girl to exclaim in embarrassment, "Oh, see here, Miriam, I'm not half so wonderful as I might be. If you said all those nice things about yourself or Grace or Anne it would be more to the point."

"But it might not be true," interposed Grace.

"And we quite agree with Miriam," added Anne.

Elfreda surveyed them in silence, an unusually tender expression in her shrewd blue eyes. "I can see that I have a whole lot to be thankful for," she said after a moment. "Next year I am going to try harder than ever to live up to your flattering opinion of me. Then I know that I can't fail to be a good senior."

Just how completely Elfreda carried out her resolution and what happened to Grace Harlowe and her friends during their senior year in college will be found in "GRACE HARLOWE'S FOURTH YEAR AT OVERTON COLLEGE."

THE END.